Terminal Agent

Jake Weidman

PREFACE

This is my story. Don't judge me too harshly. You never know what you'd do under similar circumstances. And don't call me a hero.

I had my reasons for doing what I did. Not entirely selfish. Not entirely altruistic. I'd prefer to be judged by objective measures. Not whether my actions were morally justifiable. Not whether you agree with my politics. But whether I was any good at my job.

While there's no official record I'm aware of, I've been told I was a highly productive asset in the Agency's experimental program. That's what matters to me, and this is my memoir so-to-speak.

I don't expect you to understand but I hope you respect my effectiveness. And I hope you can relate to my story. I'm just an average American given an unusual opportunity. I'm still not sure whether the Agency manipulated me but I don't regret joining the program. It broke up the monotony of my life. It gave me purpose when I stared into the abyss.

By sharing my story and breaching protocol, the bureaucrats at the Agency won't believe it but I'm grateful for the opportunity. You'll just have to trust me.

The Agency won't acknowledge my existence much less endorse my story. In fact, they'll deny 'employing' me and will deny all aspects of my story.

But I'm getting ahead of things. As there's an end, there's a beginning.

Terminal Agent 21

THE BEGINNING

You know when you look good and I looked good.

Tan. Tightly trimmed goatee. Thick, brown hair slicked back.
Piercing baby blues hidden behind tinted Aviators.

The music helped set the mood. The Doors' Roadhouse Blues played
on the radio as I exited the black, Chevy Camaro.

It was weird. I was dying but I'd never felt more alive.

Of course, intense sex with Tracy 30 minutes before may have had
something to do with it. I met Tracy eight months earlier.
Exactly six weeks after my diagnosis.

Just as I was transitioning from the first phase of grief. I met
Tracy in a stereotypical suburban bar where middle-age men and
women self-medicate to cope with their dashed hopes and dreams.

I was devastated for five weeks after the diagnosis. Twelve
months to live. No cure. Deal with it.

I dealt with it by crying a lot, missing work and lashing out.
Then I decided to 'enjoy' myself. What did I have to lose?

I'd only slept with eight women in my life. Five before marrying
Eileen. Three since our divorce. Still not sure why we divorced.
Drifted apart I guess.

It wasn't because I was unfaithful. Sure I had fantasies like
every other man with a pulse but I never acted on them while we
were married.

Now it was different. By week six, I was on the prowl. Chasing
anything and everything. From hot cougars to mediocre 30 year-
olds. Some had hail damage but nice faces. Others were hard to
make eye contact with but had other assets to compensate for
asymmetrical facial features and crooked teeth.

I didn't like using the women. I can only ascribe my compulsive
behavior as an attempt to deny my fate. Besides, I'm not sure if

I was using them or they were using me. Whatever the case, Tracy hit on me.

In hindsight, I should have been skeptical. Tracy was a 10. Thirty-year old brunette. Rockin' bod. Intense green eyes and a seductive, smoky voice.

Didn't matter at the time. Despite being 38 years old and approaching the back nine so to speak, I was fit and on a roll. I assumed she was into me.

It was the best sex I'd had since Eileen and I first started dating. Tracy made me forget I was dying. Her schedule was flexible and I made it a priority to meet with her.

Then, a month into our 'relationship,' Tracy told me the truth. Or at least the version of the truth at that time.

She worked for CIA. Tracy said the Agency could use someone in my circumstances. I thought I was being punked -- but there I was walking down a non-descript street in the bland sunniness of Jacksonville, Florida. Strolling down the boulevard on my way to my first job.

JOB 1

"What's the most important thing you're going to do?" Tracy asked, still a little breathless from ... well, I'd call it lovemaking but we both knew that would be a lie.

Staring at the water-stained ceiling of the dingy motel room, I said, "Don't say anything. Start shooting."

"Yes. And don't linger."

"Don't linger."

"I'll be waiting outside."

"You'll be waiting outside."

Tracy propped herself up on her elbow and frowned at me, "Are you finished?" The bed sheet slid down her chest, revealing one of her firm breasts.

"Yes. I'm finished."

Tracy laid her head back down on the cheap pillow.

I asked, "You're sure he'll be there?"

"I'm not going to answer that again."

"What if I'm caught?"

Tracy sighed. "We've covered this but I'll humor you because you made me ... well ..."

I smiled. Proud.

"Use your alias, Bob Bishop."

"Not Ben Morgan?"

Tracy ignored my rhetorical question. "And lawyer up. Don't answer any questions. Call the lawyer, wait and the Agency will get you out within four hours."

"And what if I'm killed?"

"You won't be."

"Humor me."

"Your mom will be notified. She'll get the life insurance and she'll get an off-the-record briefing."

"She won't understand."

Tracy snuggled up next to me. I put my arm around her as she rested her soft brunette head on my shoulder.

"She may not at first but eventually she'll understand you wanted to help your country in a truly heroic way."

"I wouldn't call it heroic."

"Of course you wouldn't."

After a pause, Tracy asked, "Have you told her about your diagnosis?"

"No. I don't want her to worry. It will be over soon enough anyway."

"Hopefully not too soon." Tracy slid her hand down my abdomen and whispered in my ear, "I'm sorry but we need to go bag a bad guy. And then we can have some more fun."

"How about a quickie now?"

"Men are all alike."

Tracy pulled the Camaro to the curb. The engine growled more like a powerboat idling than the tame purr of a high-performance car engine.

Tracy looked hot. Pink tank top. White mini-skirt. Black heels.

I felt like I was in high school again. Only difference now, I was the star. The stud.

While I was a solid contributor to my high school basketball team - enough to walk on at a D-1 school - I wasn't Mr. Basketball from my home state. When I was with Tracy, I felt

like the MVP, homecoming king *and* valedictorian. I felt
invincible.

As I closed the car door, I didn't feel any fear. Any anxiety.
Any doubt.

I felt excitement. I didn't realize how much I missed
competitive sports until I embarked on this journey.

As I walked down the street toward my first job, I felt
privileged. Like I was some sort of super-civil servant. A
human exterminator. Ridding the world of human pests.

In this case, the target was the largest meth distributor in the
Southeastern United States. Out of a dingy comic book store, Dax
Didero presided over a multi-million-drug dollar empire.

Not a high value national security target but the Agency wanted
to see if I could kill. The way I saw it, I needed practice. It
didn't matter who the targets were as long as they were bad and
deserved to die. Well ... were bad. And preferably not any
female targets.

I said no child targets and indicated a strong preference for
male targets only. I had standards after all.

Target #1 fit my profile. Bad. Guy.

The briefings indicated Target #1 started small by giving away
free samples of his product to comic book customers. All it took
for most was a taste and they were hooked, willing to do
anything to eliminate the tweaking that follows a meth high. The
compulsion to stay high destroyed families and devastated
communities.

Despite his innocuous cover as a small business owner, the
briefing indicated Target #1 was ruthless -- hiring the
requisite muscle to do whatever necessary to protect his empire.
Now the emperor was about to be dethroned. And I was the man for
the coup d'état.

Only months earlier, before my diagnosis, my greatest excitement
was negotiating a plea bargain from a petty criminal. As a

prosecutor in the suburbs of mid-Western city, I tried the occasional murder case or felony but mostly I pled out B&E and mid-level drug distribution cases. The money sucked, which put a strain on my marriage to Eileen, but I had a lot of autonomy.

Now I was five minutes from killing a man. Maybe more depending on how things went down.

Playing chicken with a bunch of underpaid, uninspired defense lawyers in bad suits seemed ... how should I put it? Trivial, to say the least, when compared to snatching life from a man.

To be truthful, I didn't know what to expect but somehow I seemed destined for this moment. Strangely prepared.

Of course, Tracy and the Agency had been 'investing' in me and I wanted to provide them with a return on their investment.

I hadn't been an idealist like Eileen but was supportive of her many causes. One thing always nagged me though. All of the complaining, ranting and pontificating of our friends at cocktail parties seemed hollow and self-serving. Devoid of any real sacrifice. Real commitment. Words. No action.

I wasn't ranting anymore. I was taking action.

Dax Did ... Dax Dider ... whatever ... Dax the drug-dealing d-bag was going to be judged and convicted by me. And the Agency.

I paused in front of the glass door to **Just Comics**. Took off my Aviators and tucked them in the lapel pocket of my black sport coat. I checked my suede Ferragamo's and pushed open the door.

As I entered, shards of sunlight illuminated my way -- penetrating the dark world of comics. And drugs.

I scanned the store. No one was there except the target. Dax was sitting at the cash register in the front as Tracy had assured me. Radiohead's ethereal anthem <u>I Might Be Wrong</u> played, adding a creepy air to the situation.

Truth be told, Dax didn't look like much of a drug-lord. Even less of a threat. He was a fat ass with a pathetic comb-over.

8

Greasy fingers, eating chicken wings and fries -- using his ill-fitting Bugs Bunny t-shirt as a napkin. He sipped a Mountain Dew and flipped through a classic comic -- some stupid Archie & Friends comic.

Despite the gentle ring of the bell when I entered, Dax didn't look up until I tapped him with the muzzle of the silencer on my Glock 45. When he looked up, I pressed the muzzle firmly against his chubby chest and pulled the trigger. The surprised expression on his bloated face faded away like suds on a plate when you rinse it.

The impact of the bullet knocked Dax back against the wall. He slid out of the aluminum chair and onto the threadbare carpet. As the fatty coughed up blood and gurgled a little, I reached over the counter and put another bullet through his head. The second slug tore a hole through the top of his skull. The thin flap of hair on top of his head wafted up then down.

I looked around the crappy store again. No one else there. Just the dead bad guy and me.

I exited.

CELEBRATION

As I walked out, Tracy pulled up in the Camaro. I opened the door. Steve Miller's <u>Take the Money & Run</u> blasted. Must have been a classic '70's station.

I got in. Tracy turned down the radio and smiled at me like I just finished a shift at Shaky's Pizza. Kind of a 'how was work, honey?' smile. I closed the car door.

"Is it done?"

"It's done."

Tracy pumped her fist. "Awesome! Good work."

Tracy was psyched. I couldn't believe how nonchalant I was.

"How do you feel?"

"Healthy."

"Good. I meant to tell you I'm not wearing panties."

I nodded. "Cool."

"That's it?"

"I'm just a little distracted."

"I'll get you to focus in 10 minutes. I can't wait any longer than that."

"What about the police? What if someone saw me get in the car?"

"That's what makes it exciting. I've got a mental checklist of what I want you to do."

I appreciated how matter-of-fact Tracy was about sex. Kiss me here. Touch me there.

The directness usually turned me on. But I only responded, "Uh, huh."

"Screw it. I can't wait. Give me your hand."

I put my hand on Tracy's thigh. She guided it to where she wanted it. A few moments later, Tracy turned up the radio and gunned it.

We were speeding down a desolate road, rock music blaring and now I was getting into it. I switched hands and leaned over, kissing Tracy's neck and right ear.

Neither of us could wait any longer. Tracy pulled the car into the parking lot of an abandoned strip mall where we could celebrate my first righteous kill.

MORE THAN SEX

It wasn't all sex and killing. There was a lot of planning to kill. A lot of weapons training and simulations, both live-action and virtual. Tracy and the Agency were training me for the ultimate job. And Tracy and I had 'fun' in the interim.

I was tutored in Russian history and current global affairs -- from a Russian perspective. The RT channel was a great resource. A steady stream of slickly presented Russian propaganda lapped up by unsuspecting US cable subscribers. And I read everything and anything, classified and unclassified, about George Ranier.

In the scheme of things, George Ranier was essentially a nobody. A nobody with access to highly sensitive information. As a US government contractor, Ranier had access to classified information regarding super-secret spy programs the National Security Agency or NSA ran against enemies and allies alike.

Ranier, a systems administrator for the NSA, leaked embarrassing and damaging information regarding the US government's massive data mining programs, revealing the government's apparent disregard for personal privacy -- not to mention the Constitution. While the intentions seemed pure -- protect America, its citizens and its allies -- the programs raised serious civil rights concerns and complicated already challenging US international relations.

I wondered, as the press speculated, whether Ranier was just a government contractor or an Agency asset who went rogue. I didn't care.

As I saw it, Ranier was a traitor. While my point of view regarding Ranier evolved as I learned more about the US surveillance programs, the fact Russia was harboring him only solidified my conclusion that Ranier was a traitor.

But I'm getting ahead of things. I had only killed one target and it was an easy kill. I later came to find out Dax wasn't a drug kingpin as I had been led to believe but a pedophile.

Being misled bothered me. Killing Dax didn't.

He deserved it and the local media said so. I provided justice for his victims and their families that the court system never could. I was proud.

DOUBTS

The Coles job would not be a walk in the park.

Ret. Lt. Colonel Herbert Coles was a badass. And he had a professional security detail -- ex-Special forces. Tracy and other members of the team meticulously prepared me for this job.

It was about this time that I started to wonder whether I was in remission, cured or whether I was ever really sick. Whether the government had used some sophisticated algorithm to identify people like me then lie to us. Something like, 'you have 12 months to live and oh, by the way, did you park in the lot? We validate.'

People who wanted to contribute. Serve a higher power. Republican-leaning, terminally ill divorcees with no children.

People, who when told they would die within a defined period of time wouldn't obsessively check off a superficial bucket list but want to serve a purpose. Some temporal objective to achieve in their dying days.

For me, I'd like to say it was love of my country but it wasn't. I simply didn't want to fade away. I wanted to contribute. To be remembered for something. Even if it was only me who remembered.

Plus, the anger phase of my grief was rather extended and the 'program' helped me channel that anger into something I viewed as productive. Maybe the Agency manipulated me, making me think I had nothing to lose so they could use me to fulfill geo-political ambitions. Or maybe the Agency gave me an opportunity.

Whatever the case, I felt great. Was it the effects of the steroid treatment the government had me taking? Was the experimental treatment working?

I was violently ill for one week after the initial treatment, recuperated for one week and since then felt better than I had in years. Whether I was still ill, ever ill or in remission, I wanted to move forward with the program.

To help prepare me, Tracy led a rigorous workout regimen, tightly controlled diet, 'special' pills, role playing (not the kind you're thinking of) and tactical training at various black sites across the globe.

Importantly, development of my cover story had started.

"Ok," Tracy began. "The Leon Black blog is taking shape. Lots of virulent content -- "

"Virulent?" I asked with a smile as we sat on the patio of a safe house in rural Virginia. It was a cool fall afternoon. Tracy wore a red and black plaid shirt, black scarf, torn jeans and cowboy boots.

"Yes, virulent."

"I wouldn't say that," shifting in my wicker chair.

"I know. It's too sophisticated for you."

"Ouch."

"Well if the boot fits ...," Tracy smiled.

She continued, "Point is, Leon Black would say that."

"Leon Black doesn't exist," I noted.

"As far as Colonel Coles, the anarchist and Ranier go, Leon Black is real. You're Leon Black."

I read from the briefing document, "Leon Black, a libertarian blogger, is embraced by extremists on both the left and the right. Some consider him an anarchist. Some consider him a fascist. All know him for his virulent ... vitriolic prose.

"Who wrote this?" I asked.

"Probably a team of junior staffers at Langley."

"Figures."

"What do you mean by that? I was one of those junior staffers."

"Well ..."

"Well, what?" Tracy asked.

" ... if the boot fits."

Tracy raised an eyebrow.

"It just seems a little affected."

"Affected? Now who sounds pretentious?" Tracy said.

"Anyway," back to the briefing, "Black is a firebrand anti-establishment figure who is hugely popular online with more than 20 million followers.

"That sounds like a lot."

"Yes. We were able to manipulate the Nielsen figures so the world believes you, I mean, Leon Black is one of the most widely followed bloggers in the world."

"Wow."

"Yeah. The crazy part is the number of actual followers is steadily trending upward."

"Nice work. Way to foment dissension."

Tracy laughed.

Reading again from the briefing, "Black's commentary ranges from economic matters, globalization, environmental degradation, immigration, international affairs, etc. He has woven together several well-researched conspiracy theories. Enough to be persuasive for his audience."

Off script, I asked, "Conspiracy theories like what?"

"They're in the briefing later but ones like the mistaken downing of the Malaysian airliner over Ukraine."

"How's that insightful? Of course, it was a mistake. Unless someone wants to stir up public opinion against themselves."

"Mistaken in that Putin flew the same route 20 minutes earlier. On his way back from the World Cup."

"A hit on Putin? Bullshit."

Tracy was expressionless.

"Like threatening to kill the Greek prime minister and his family if he pursued an oil pipeline with Russia."

"No way."

"I don't know. You tell me Leon.

"Prime Minister Kostas Karamanlis, an incredibly popular politician, withdraws from public eye and prematurely calls for parliamentary elections, the result of which is the election of George Papandreou, who doesn't even hold a Greek passport. Only an American one. Upon election, Papandreou, cancels the Russian deal and defaults on Greece's sovereign debt, throwing Greece to the European wolves."

"That's crazy. It doesn't make any sense that --"

"I don't know, your people lap it up." Tracy laughed.

I shook my head, "This is getting weird. We created a blogger out of thin air. Put together fake content."

Tracy grimaced.

"Put out false trending data and bang, we have a shit-load of followers."

"Yep."

"Amazing."

Turning back to the briefing, "So fascists and commies both embrace me."

"Yes. The economic data cited by Leon is used by both the left and the right to push their agendas."

"What kind of data?"

"Like a Cap Gemini study asserting that the world's wealthiest 1%, a mere 15 million people out of nearly 7 billion people on earth, will soon control $70 trillion."

"That sounds like a lot."

"Sure does. It's that kind of wealth concentration that scares both the left and the right."

"Well, turns out I'm not a divider, I am a unifier."

"Don't let it go to your head. We just want you to be able to get face to face with a few key targets."

I nodded, "Of course. Especially the ultimate assignment."

"Yes. Ranier."

"Well. I'm the man for the job."

"Well. Not quite. But we're getting there.

"It's not just about your circumstances. I mean, no offense, but there are lots of folks dying."

"None taken," I said. A little hurt.

"I mean ... the US government doesn't invest millions of dollars on everyone with your condition."

"Millions of dollars?"

"Don't you think I'm worth it?" Tracy said. Her turn to feel hurt.

"Of course. I mean -- "

"Don't worry about it. But yes, millions of dollars when you consider the training, the travel expenses, the elaborate cover stories being developed ... and yes, me."

"Why not just cure me?"

"We would if we could."

"That's not true."

"What do you mean?"

"I mean, the government is expecting a return on its investment. You don't want me cured."

"Don't be ridiculous."

"I'm not being ridiculous. If I was cured, you wouldn't have a way to manipulate me. You only need me to remain healthy enough to do the job. But not be cured."

"You can leave anytime. You know that."

"I know. I'm just saying maybe I was never ill."

"I'm not having that conversation again," Tracy said.

"Of course not."

"What? What do you want me to say?" Tracy was agitated.

"Did the Agency identify you from your online profile?"

"Well?"

"Well what?"

"You know, data mining," I said.

"Like mining data using algorithms for logistic regression and cluster analysis, looking for anomalies and dependencies?"

"Well ... " I stammered.

"Like applying enhanced K-means and orthogonal partitioning to relational, transaction, object-oriented, spatial, and active databases, as well as global information systems?"

"Yeah. That."

"To extract information from a data lake and transform it into an understandable structure for further use?"

"Hey. This sounds pretty specific. Are you disagreeing with me or confirming my suspicions?"

"Neither.

"Like I said. I'm not having this conversation again."

"Whatever. I guess we're all getting something out of this arrangement."

"I certainly hope so."

"I'm just saying. Because I have nothing left to lose, I'm a unique asset."

Tracy didn't respond.

"Unique because I'm dying and I'm anonymous. No wife. No children. No loose ends."

Tracy looked out at the Oak trees in the back yard. The color of their leaves was changing. The afternoon sun was fading.

TRACY

We completed the day's 'lessons' and sat quietly. It was getting a bit chilly. I zipped up my leather jacket.

Tracy scrolled through her playlist for a song. She selected The Other Side by the Rhett Walker band. A song about sin, death and redemption. Seemed an appropriate ballad given our line of work – at least the sin and death part.

I could tell Tracy was boring with me. The sex dwindled. Not the same passion.

As I contemplated that sad fact, I realized I knew virtually nothing about Tracy. She knew nearly everything about me.

Where I went to elementary school. No siblings. My favorite sports teams – Bears and Cubs. What my hobbies were – golf and golf. Used to be golf and hoops. That my dad committed suicide when I was in high school. All sorts of facts.

Of course, reading a dossier and experiencing life with someone are two entirely different things. The former an academic, antiseptic exercise.

The other, real. Messy. Requires emotional investment. Time. Attention. Shared pain. Suffering. Joy. Sadness.

Anyway, I felt guilty I didn't know anything about Tracy. Check that. I felt guilty I hadn't even wondered until now. I guess I was wrapped up in my own shit.

I hadn't considered Tracy as a person. More of an avatar in a virtual world than a living, breathing person.

"How did you end up at the Agency?"

"Well I'm not terminal if that's what you mean."

I was taken aback.

"I'm sorry. I didn't mean it like that."

"OK."

21

"They identified me at MIT."

"Impressive."

"Well it wasn't all cotton candy and pony rides."

"What do you mean?"

"Let's just say I didn't have a middle-America upbringing.

"My parents were deadhead drifters unfit to raise me and my little brother per the courts. So we were sent to foster care. If that wasn't bad enough, they separated us."

"I'm sorry."

"Yeah. So am I.

"Foster care was terrible and I was rebellious to say the least. I wouldn't have made it if it wasn't for a high school teacher who took an interest in me. Believed in me.

"Turns out my parents were fuck-ups but they happened to be extremely intelligent. I got some of that. Enough to get a perfect score on the SATs. Got in to MIT and the rest is history."

"That's amazing."

"Well. I left some things out."

"Like what?"

"College is when I first demonstrated nymphomania characteristics."

I felt like a creep.

"I slept with my professors. Both men ... and women.

"I got really drunk at a party sophomore year. Some chick was hitting on my physics prof. I smoked a lot of pot with him and occasionally slept with him -- mainly around exam time. Anyway, I beat the shit out of the chick ... and the burnout prof as well.

"It's still a little fuzzy. I had blacked out."

"Wow."

"Yeah. That's what the university said.

"They expelled me and pressed charges. It was jail or the Agency for me."

"How so?"

"Turns out CIA had identified me a few years before. Apparently, I fit some profile."

I nodded. "I know what you mean."

Tracy managed a smile.

"You had your own anger management issues, didn't you?"

"How so?"

"The agency knows everything."

I just looked at Tracy.

"The stockbroker you beat within an inch of his life?"

Tracy was referring to a stockbroker who bilked my family out of all of our money. Drove my father to suicide. Even though I believed the arrest had been expunged from my record with the help of a friend. Obviously, I was wrong.

"Oh that," I said.

"Yes, that."

We listened to the song for a few minutes. Then I spoke.

"What happened to your little brother?"

"He died of a drug overdose two years ago."

"I'm sorry."

"Me too." The song ended.

THE RANIER DOSSIER

Whether or not Tracy was becoming bored with me, she remained dedicated to my preparation. To ensure I had a comprehensive, 360 view of Ranier, Tracy tutored me on third-party accounts of Ranier and his exploits as well as the Agency's official briefing. The idea was to remove any unintended bias so that my eventual interaction with the target would be as authentic as possible.

Whatever you might think of the Agency, they went to lengths in briefings to be factual -- other than the Dax job, which was essentially a pass/fail test of whether I could kill or not. The Agency wouldn't risk any exposure on a newbie like me without knowing I could fulfill the basic job requirement - killing another person. Someone who deserved it, of course.

Anyway, to be effective, you needed facts not propaganda. Consequently, my reading list included Pulitzer prize winning accounts of Ranier and his betrayal, or depending on your perspective, self-less act.

After challenging myself and researching the matter, I concluded Ranier had to pay for his betrayal - the most damaging intelligence leak in US history.

"I think reasonable people could agree that Ranier had other options," I said. "Why jeopardize the safety of millions of Americans and citizens of other countries just because you can? Why not go through official channels? Or at least try?"

"Hell, take it to the Department of Justice." Tracy mimicked. "Or your Congressperson for fuck sake."

I ignored Tracy's mocking of me.

"Ranier supposedly asserted that he didn't want to live in a world where all of his thoughts, words, dreams were subject to scrutiny by the government - an invasion of privacy - specifically by the NSA.

25

"While I empathize with that sentiment, it's misleading. The NSA mined nameless, faceless metadata – the epitome of raw data – looking for patterns."

"So your saying, to believe your thoughts, words, dreams are uniquely of interest to the NSA or anyone other than your friends and family is narcissistic?"

"Yes. To say the least.

"Like you and me, our thoughts, words, dreams, etc. are random, homogenous, meaningless bits and bites flowing in a nearly immeasurable sea of anonymous data."

"So there are no risks?"

"There are risks but in a democratic society such as ours with checks and balances, appropriate monitoring and oversight is possible in my view.

"Whatever the case, don't kid yourself; the only way to protect against devastating terrorist attacks is prevention. The targets are innumerable and too diverse to stop once in action. Only preventative measures are effective. Plus, do you believe our enemies don't have similar programs? Do you trust the US democratic system less than Russia? China?"

"True."

"At the end of the day, the way I see it, who the hell was he. I'd have been more sympathetic if Ranier didn't have a chip on his shoulder."

"How so?" Tracy asked.

"As reported by those sympathetic to Ranier, at 18 years of age, he described himself as belligerent and self-important with no respect for elders. Not too much of a stretch to conclude he was a narcissistic computer genius who thought he knew better than everyone else. Like I said, who the hell was he?"

"So tell me how you really feel," Tracy said.

"What a lack of humility. A sanctimonious, smug little prick. A product of an over-indulgent society."

2014
Jake Weidman

"Alright. Enough. You'd made your point," Tracy said.

To prepare for an eventual in person meet with Ranier, Tracy and the team also quizzed me on Japanese culture. For some reason, Ranier was obsessed with all things Japanese.

Seriously, how far do some people go to be different? To stand out the from the crowd. To create an identity.

I'm not a psychologist, but a middleclass American with Ranier's tastes had to be an indication of some sort of syndrome. Clearly, he was trying to fill some kind of void.

The preparations included one trip to Tokyo and three virtual trips. The in-person trip was important. When role playing or playing a part, actually experiencing something helped you be convincing.

Our latest preparation took place while we were on the road, staying at a non-descript hotel on the outskirts of Pittsburgh. It was one of those extended stay places where we had a kitchenette and small 'family room.'

"What's your favorite place in Tokyo?" Tracy asked.

"The Shinto shrines are awesome and the buzz of Shibuya Crossing is addicting but Yoyogi Park on a weekend is the best."

"Why?"

"Beautiful park and great for people watching. Everything goes there, which is a cool contrast with the stereotypical reserved Japanese culture.

"You'll see old people exercising. Teenagers skateboarding. Couples sharing wine and cheese. You name it."

"Wow. You sound like you actually like Japan."

Breaking character, I said, "Actually, I found Tokyo really impressive. It's one of the most populated cities in the world but the city seems so manageable.

"Other than anime, which I don't get, it's a pretty hip, interesting place."

"Don't go for Japanese-style animation?"

"No. It's lame."

"Favorite Japanese cuisine?"

"Sushi with cold Saki."

"Favorite Saki?"

"Ah. Hard to find but worth the effort. Nabeshima from the Fukuchiyo Shuzo brewery in the Saga prefecture."

Tracy nodded.

"Well done."

"Now how about opening your kimono," I asked.

Tracy smiled, got up and walked towards the bedroom.

I waited a few minutes, trying not to seem too eager. In reality, I probably waited 20 seconds.

THE RACIST

Ret. Colonel Coles, former lieutenant colonel in the United States Marine Corps, was the self-proclaimed emancipator of the white man. He was the leader of the latest version of neo-Nazism or Aryanism American style.

Tracy briefed me on Colonel Coles.

"So the guy went from being a career Marine to the leader of antigovernment zealots," I said.

"Well, he's not the first and probably won't be the last," Tracy said. "Remember McVeigh and Nichols?"

"Yeah, that's true. Still, I just don't understand how you can go from one extreme to the other. From faithfully serving one's country to despising its government and forming the so-called Fourth Reich."

"When push comes to shove, I think most of these guys have petty personal gripes rather than some grand political ideology. They're just bitter."

"Maybe. Whatever the case, this psycho is bitter enough to persuade and lead 150 or so followers, although apparently only 50 are loyalists with the remainder just sympathizers."

Tracy pulled some photos out of a hard copy file and spread them out on the table.

"This simple log-framed building is the Fourth Reich's mess hall. There are several other buildings and cabins where the members live."

I reviewed the photos.

Tracy said, "We believe the Colonel relies on the Fourth Reich's so-called Elite Corp to gather intelligence and conduct the Fourth Reich's clandestine operations. Discussions of strategy appear to be reserved for the Elite Corp, a team of five lieutenants."

Reading from the briefing, I noted, "Coles believes America has been imploding since the Civil War. That a leftist media sicks Big Government on the social problem de jour while the 'huddled masses,' the 'silent majority,' get manipulated. Conditioned. Much like Pavlov's dog."

"Well, so far..." I smiled.

"Real funny," Tracy said.

Continuing, I read, "He asserts there is no freedom left. Democracy is a joke. The tail is wagging the dog."

I flipped the page. "Here's an excerpt from one of his diatribes."

"Per Coles, 'Thomas Jefferson would roll over in his grave if knew the extent to which the federal government permeates the average American's life.

'A small cabal of financiers own America's capital resources, the Harvard WASPS run the government, and the underclass keeps sawing the legs off the table so that the middle class, the backbone of America, has to eat its meals with the dogs.

'Well, no more. We're going to put a stop to the madness. We are going to systematically dismantle America and rebuild it based on the white, Anglo-Saxon model the country was founded upon.'"

"Well alrighty then," I said.

Tracy laughed but said, "It would be funny except this guy is effective and the Agency and the FBI believe there's a connection between the senior Senator from the State of South Carolina and Coles."

"It may explain the timely interruptions in our surveillance per the briefing," I said.

"It has to be someone with real pull. Someone in the military-industrial establishment. A big-time military contractor or Pentagon brass," Tracy said.

"Or a US Senator?"

"Someone able to clean dirty money so well that neither the FBI nor the IRS could trace the large sums of dough that freely flows in and out of the Fourth Reich's bank accounts."

I said, "Maybe being the second ranking member on the Senate Commerce Committee has it perks."

"Yeah but does the Chairman of the Senate Arms Committee, have the ability to selectively turn the national defense radar system on and off at his convenience? Just long enough to allow the Colonel's jet to slip through the web of radar covering the continental United States?"

"Doubtful," I said.

"I agree. Either way, every time the FBI loses contact with the Colonel and his cohorts their disappearance seems to be followed shortly by front-page headlines.

Tracy read from the briefing, "Local Radio Talk-Show Host Gunned Down - Anti-Semitism Suspected"; "Black Congressman Shot to Death -- Motive Unclear"; "Southern Baptist Leadership Conferee Dies in Suspicious Car Crash."

"This guy sounds like a serious threat."

"That's why he's on the list," Tracy said.

JUMP

My living arrangement was erratic.

I sold my home upon joining the program. Gave the money to my mom. Told her it was a bonus for winning a big case. She was grateful and asked no questions other than whether I could afford it. Self-less as always.

We had struggled for money since my father committed suicide. Killed himself after losing all of our savings in a get rich quick deal that turned out to be a ponzi scheme. If the humiliation of being fleeced wasn't enough, my mom's shame pushed him over the edge.

While no mom is perfect and mine certainly wasn't, I was grateful for her. I loved her. And I admired her perseverance – particularly after my father's suicide. St. Paul in his Epistles says trials teach us perseverance and perseverance leads to hope. And hope leads to faith.

I reassured her that I could afford it and I prayed for continued hope. Hope in a future. Hope in a loving God. Hope in a life hereafter. I was counting on it – even if I pushed it from my thoughts as I pursued the program with vigor.

_____

Since selling the house, the Agency shuttled me to and from safe houses and uninspiring motels. The kind of motels you find on the perimeter of architecturally uninspiring office parks, where powdered eggs and mediocre coffee are included in the room rate.

Sometimes Tracy accompanied me, increasingly in an adjoining room instead of sharing a room like in the beginning. Other times I was on my own, which I was starting to prefer.

I was beginning to view the program as a profession and I wanted to focus. My health seemed stable. Increasingly in the back of my mind, which was a relief.

Bottom line: if I was going to play the game, I wanted to be a starter. I was nearly six months into the program and wanted to progress faster. If that meant less intimacy with Tracy, so be it. I wanted to eliminate national security threats.

I didn't want to be limited to fat fucks like Dax and I was increasingly concerned I'd be relegated to playing the role of a high school jock, who mistakenly believes being the high school star is the apex of a lifetime. I didn't want anything or anyone holding me back - even if that meant weaning myself from Tracy.

I got my chance on a crisp, moonlit fall night on the outskirts of Denver. I was staying at a non-descript motel like all the road warrior salesmen and women who crisscross middle America Monday through Thursday.

I was awakened at 02.00 by a knock on the door. I instinctively retrieved my Glock from beneath the mattress. I quietly moved toward the door. I didn't tiptoe straight to the door but crept into the adjacent bathroom.

As I leaned on the bathroom door, I realized how the training was paying off. I didn't hurry. I didn't delay. I calmly retrieved my weapon and methodically made my way to the relative safety of the bathroom. My breathing was deep and steady.

"Yes," I evenly responded.

"It's Martha. I'm with the Agency," a voice from the hallway answered.

"What do you want?"

"I need your help. It's urgent."

"Confirm."

"You're Bob Bishop. You work closely with Tracy."

"Then why isn't she here?"

"She's on assignment elsewhere ... we need to leave now."

"What's the code word?"

"Omaha."

I put on the bathrobe hanging on the back of the bathroom door
then opened the door.

HOW HIGH?

In the next 10 minutes, I found myself speeding through the nearby low-rise suburban office park with a woman I didn't know at the wheel of a black Range Rover. Surprisingly, I wasn't wigged out.

Martha spoke quickly but calmly. That helped. Some operatic song played. I later learned that the appropriate word is 'aria.'

"There's a situation," Martha said as she stared intently at the road.

Martha wasn't as attractive as Tracy but she was pretty in a sophisticated kind of way. Looked to be mid-30's. Blue eyes, high cheekbones and a prominent nose, which I found attractive. Martha had her dishwater blond hair in a ponytail. She looked like a hot lawyer.

"It's going to be dangerous."

"OK."

"There's been a kidnapping."

"Isn't that the domain of the FBI?"

Martha broke her focus on the winding road to glare at me.

Eyes back on the road, "In 10 minutes, we're going to pull into the parking lot of ICG Corporation. It's a cloud company.

"Headquarters are in San Francisco but they maintain thousands of servers and satellites here in the Mile High City. Denver is almost equally positioned between Europe and Asia hence the significant number of satellite farms. Only one bounce and you have worldwide coverage."

"Are we buying gigabytes of storage?"

Martha ignored my attempt at levity. Note to self. Reminded me of Martha from the Martha and Mary Bible story.

"ICG's CEO, Peter Gruber, spends a lot of time in the Denver office because he has a place in Aspen. Mr. Gruber has been kidnapped.

"It's off the grid. Not even the FBI knows about it."

"What do the kidnappers want?"

"To bring down the US banking system."

"How'd the Agency find out?"

"Data mining."

Sounded like confirmation of the programs Ranier disclosed.

"Alright. What's the plan?"

"We're going to kill the kidnappers and free the CEO."

"OK."

Martha pulled into the parking lot.

"The security guard will let us in. We'll then work our way up to the CEO's office on the 5th floor. Southwest corner.

"Just follow my lead. And trust your training."

We parked the car in the loading dock in the rear of the building. Before we exited the car, Martha opened the glove box and pulled out two pair of infrared goggles. She handed one to me. They were goofy looking. Kind of like swim goggles. But they weren't bulky and stayed on tight.

We exited the car. The security guard let us in the back entrance as Martha had indicated. The guard explained that he thought there were two gunmen. He said the gunmen must have entered during the day. There was no forced entry after hours.

The layout was open-plan with a large atrium in the middle of the building and conference rooms outlining the perimeter. Two bridges connected the two halves of the office floors split by the atrium, which made our approach tricky and dangerous.

Using the elevators or bridges would leave us exposed. The security guard recommended the southeast stairwell opposite the CEO's corner office as our best option.

We kibitzed at the security guard's desk on the 1st floor. To create a possible diversion, Martha instructed the security guard to send all of the elevators to the 5th floor in 10 minutes – hopefully synchronized with our arrival on five via the stairwell. Then Martha asked the security guard, "Does the intercom work?"

"Yeah. I think so. Why?"

Martha handed the guard her mobile. Moments later "Giusto ciel! In tal periglio" from Rossini's L'Assedio di Corinto began to play. She said to turn it up louder in 10 minutes.

As if the situation wasn't surreal enough, we started our journey upward to the haunting aria. Martha would later explain that in the aria, the women of Corinth are pleading to God for help as the city prepares for invasion by the Ottomans.

Martha slowly opened the door to the southeast corner of the fifth floor. We duck-walked our way out of the stairwell to a row of nearby cubicles. Martha quietly closed the door behind us.

Martha motioned for me to move towards the southwest corner office along the perimeter wall on the left while she was going to slide to the right and then converge on the office at a 45-degree angle.

Martha whispered, "Follow my lead. Shoot to kill. Our #1 objective is to neutralize the bad guys."

I nodded. Message received. Kill the bad people. Saving the CEO would be a happy byproduct but an acceptable loss if necessary.

Poor CEO. He'd better hope we were good. Otherwise, this would be his last night as CEO of a cloud company and he'd become a resident of the cloud ... city. Never mind. Only good news for

him was that the security guard said the CEO was wearing a
Hawaiian shirt – apparently a Jimmy Buffet Margarita Ville
parrot-head.

We pulled on our night vision goggles and made our way to the
corner office. I squatted as I made my way along the perimeter.
I was approximately 25 feet away from the office. We had a good
view in because the walls were floor to ceiling glass. Only wood
was the door, which was open.

As I steadily progressed toward the door, I periodically caught
a glimpse of Martha as she moved directly toward the office.
When we were approximately 20 feet from the office, the
elevators arrived and the music volume increased. One of the
gunman peered out the doorway. He was Asian.

Martha didn't hesitate. On one knee she expertly placed two
bullets in the gunman's forehead. He dropped like a string.
Martha and I moved closer.

Moments later, the second gunman exited with the CEO tightly in
his grip, gun to his head. The gunman had his left arm wrapped
under the CEO's arms and held the gun to the CEO's head with his
right hand.

The gunman scanned the floor looking for us but he didn't see
us. Then he started to scream in Mandarin, as I was later
advised. I couldn't understand a word but later found it
humorous how he had to shout to be heard over the music.

In any case, I didn't have a clear shot. Nor did Martha but that
didn't stop her. Again, without hesitation, Martha quickly fired
two bullets into the gunman's right elbow, essentially severing
his arm in two and preventing him from pulling the trigger. The
gun dropped from his hand.

As the gunman reeled in pain, he let go of the CEO and stumbled
back against the doorframe. I now had a clear shot. I fired one
bullet in his temple as Martha fired another one into his
forehead, redecorating the doorway to the CEO's office with the
gunman's brains and skull.

We quickly moved in. The CEO had fallen to the floor and was
crawling to safety. We pulled him up.

38

Martha didn't say a word as she led him to the stairwell.
Without a word, she led him down the stairs and back to the
loading dock where a black van waited. We loaded the disoriented
CEO up and the van pulled away.

Pretty damn efficient.

TAKING OUT THE GARBAGE (AGAIN)

The post-event debrief was just that. Brief.

Immediately after the van pulled away, Martha and I got in the Range Rover and left the ICG premises. Martha made a call as we pulled out of the parking lot.

Lots of 'yes's' and 'no's'.

"Security tapes? Yes. On-site team secured them."

Martha hung up. The call lasted less than a minute.

"We'll debrief later. Something has come up. An opportunity."

"Yes?" My entire life was opportunistic at this point.

Martha explained that the head of one of Mexico's biggest drug cartels was in the US. "It's a short window and you and I are the closest. It's on the West coast."

"So there are others?"

"What others?"

"Other teams. Other assets like me."

"Look who has a high opinion of themselves."

"I'm just saying."

"Saying what?"

"Saying that there are others."

"I didn't say that."

"You implied that."

Martha ignored my comment. I was confident there were other agents like me. Surely the Agency wouldn't bet on just one horse.

We drove in silence for 15 minutes, when Martha announced, "We're here."

We pulled up to the gates of a county airport. The security guard waived us through.

Martha pulled the car up to a Gulfstream G550. Stairs down.

We exited the car and boarded the jet. I never knew whether these were government jets or private jets leased by the Agency but they were posh.

After taxi and takeoff the briefing began without any introduction from Martha. It was the two pilots and us. Martha and I sat in comfortable captains seats across the aisle from each other. I opened a bottled water and sipped from it, compliments of US taxpayers I presumed.

"We have a unique opportunity to take out the head of the Juarez cartel, Miguel Lopez. He and his wife are visiting universities in the US this week."

To protect the innocent, I won't name the university where the action would take place but let's just say some refer to it as the 'Harvard of the West.'

Anyway, there was one disturbing fact and Martha had only begun the briefing.

"Wife?" I interrupted.

"Yes. Wife. Is that a problem?"

"I don't know if you read my application but I specifically said no child targets and preferably no women."

Martha remained stoic despite my wit. "Their son won't be with them."

"I get that but the wife will be, correct?"

"Correct."

I sighed and looked out the window. "What if I decline?"

"You're done with the program. I leave you in California and we thank you for your service."

I wanted to say 'and you'll kill me' (again, no loose ends) but
I didn't. Instead, I said, "You don't have that authority."

"I do."

"I want to talk with Tracy."

"She's not available and she can't help anyway. It's my call."

"What about the treatment? Would that continue?"

"Doubtful," Martha responded coldly.

"What about Alan Munger?" Alan was the name of my Langley
contact. Met with him every six weeks for psyche and physical
evals. And treatment.

"Alan can't help either. It's my call."

"I still want to speak with him." This wasn't my first rodeo.

"Fine but by the time you speak with him we'll have scrambled
another team."

"Another team. There you go again."

No response from Martha.

"I thought we're the closest."

"Closet team. Yes.

"But this is a high value target and we would use an F-16 if
necessary to transport the asset."

Check.

"So I have no choice _if_ I want to stay in the program ... _and_
continue to receive treatment?"

"Correct."

Check mate.

"I guess I should have read the fine print." I didn't care if
Martha wouldn't bite on my attempts at humor and she didn't.

"If it makes you feel better, Carlos' wife is a real piece of work."

"Yeah?"

"Yeah."

Martha pulled out a laptop from her canvas Tumi briefcase, opened it and logged on. Once logged on, Martha turned the screen towards me so I could see. She scrolled down the file folder and clicked on a file named '1112.' The file opened up a video sequence.

"This footage was secretly taken by an informant inside the organization."

I leaned forward. The grainy video was shot inside a warehouse. Martha turned up the audio.

The camera zoomed in on a lone figure tied to a chair in the middle of the warehouse. His shirt was soaked in blood, which dripped from his cheeks and chin.

I squinted at the screen and it appeared one of his eyes had been gauged out. While I don't speak Spanish, it seemed as though he was pleading. Pleading for mercy.

Off-camera a shrill voice screamed back at him, periodically interrupted by maniacal cackles. Enter stage left Senora Lopez.

Ms. Lopez strutted toward the man in the chair. She was wearing knee-high black leather boots, tight leather shorts and a bra. The sick scene was some sort of sadistic play and Ms. Lopez was both the director and the antagonist.

Referring to the man in the chair, Martha said, "He's a capo from a rival cartel." I could only manage to nod.

Ms. Lopez circled behind the victim, stopped behind him and leaned down to whisper in his ear. Then she slowly raised a mirror up to the man's face. He screamed in horror.

Martha nonchalantly said, "The Mexican gangs staple back your eyelids so you have to look." I felt sick to my stomach and turned away.

2014
Jake Weidman

Martha closed the laptop. After a few moments, she said, "Well?"

I shook my head and took a deep breath, trying to cleanse my mind if that were possible.

"What's the set up?"

LIKE THE SLOGAN SAYS, JUST DO IT (JOBS 2 AND 3)

The set up for jobs 2 and 3 was simple. I was posing as Bob Schmidt – the admissions officer Carlos and Juanita were planning to meet to discuss little junior cartel boss' college application. The meeting was scheduled for 07.30 followed by a tour of the campus, including an introduction to the university provost.

I can only assume the university had no idea who they were dealing with. To be fair, Senor Lopez had gone to great lengths to create a legitimate public persona – something Michael Corleone was unable to achieve. I guess with enough money (the Agency estimated $1.5 billion) even evil criminals can create a false public persona. But $1.5 billion? So much for the war on drugs.

Our plane touched down 04.00 PST at a private airstrip near the university. Martha and I arrived at the campus at 06.00 after freshening up at a nearby motel.

We arrived in a black SUV and waited for a local agent. As we waited, I asked, "What about the real Bob Schmidt?"

"He's been detained by the local police on child endangerment charges. We've sent in a phony defense attorney who will keep him incommunicado until we've wrapped up here."

"He didn't do anything," I said.

"Don't worry. Charges will be dropped. All a big mistake, etc. Mr. Schmidt will be relieved."

"Yeah but – "

"You have to break eggs to make an omelet."

"That's all you can come up with? A weak cliché."

"Hey. I'm kind of busy if you haven't noticed."

"Too busy to care about – "

"And he won't go to the press. He doesn't want the stench of false allegations following him." Martha was having none of it.

I shook my head. "Kind of like the old 'when did you stop beating your wife?' lawyer trick question."

"Exactly. Mr. Schmidt will have one day living in a Kafka novel and then go on with his life."

"What about the university? Aren't they going to ask questions?"

"No one wants bad publicity. The cloud company has an impending IPO. Last thing they wanted was for the public to know about their security breach. The university is no different."

"Other than the fact that the parents of a prospective student are killed while visiting the school. That can't be good for recruiting."

"Yeah but would they rather be known as the school that recruits the offspring of tyrants, oligarchs and brutal drug lords?"

"I suppose not."

"And no civil lawsuit because the dead people are criminals."

"Nice and tidy," I added.

Martha continued, "Yep. The local papers will say a depressed admissions officer, not a stretch, kills parents of future student and then himself. Agency uses the body of a homeless man from the local morgue as the so-called 'admissions officer' and we all move on."

"Just like that."

"Yes. Just like that."

"Except for Carlos and his wife."

"Yes. If you do your job."

The local agent let me into the admission's office before anyone else arrived so I could get settled in Mr. Schmidt's office. Once seated at the desk, I placed one of my Glocks in the top

right drawer and the other under some papers on the desk. Mr.
Schmidt wasn't OCD so there were plenty of miscellaneous papers
strewn about his desk.

I was the first person to enter the administration offices. The
Lopez' had requested an early meeting consistent with their
desire to keep a low profile. This request significantly reduced
potential collateral damage. Half-hour later our guests of honor
arrived.

Senor and Senorita Lopez' beast of a bodyguard accompanied them
to the door. He was built like the Rock but lacked his grace and
good looks.

I reached out to shake Mr. Lopez' hand. He simply nodded. Hands
remaining in the pockets of his pinstriped suit. No eye contact.

He entered the office and walked past me. I dropped my hand and
smiled at him and Ms. Lopez, inviting them into 'my office.'

Ms. Lopez was attractive. Olive skin. Jet black, shoulder-length
hair. She wore a smart blue suit and high but tasteful heels.
The grainy video didn't do her justice.

Unlike her husband, Ms. Lopez looked directly at me. Her round,
brown eyes intently scrutinizing my blue ones. Recalling the
brutal scene Martha showed me, I have to admit feeling unsettled
upon meeting the villainess from the video.

"Please come in," I said. My voice slightly quivered.

"Gracias," Mr. Lopez said, finally glancing at me.

"Please have a seat."

As they started to take a seat, Ms. Lopez said, "You look
different from your Facebook page."

The bodyguard, who had been closing the door, stopped in the
doorway.

So much for a tight set up. I sensed she'd made me.

"Well, you know. Pictures can be deceiving."

"Gorge, please join us," Ms. Lopez directed the bodyguard.

Gorge stepped back into the room and closed the door.

Ms. Lopez wouldn't relent.

"You really do look different than your Facebook page."

"The picture was taken a while ago."

"How long ago?"

She definitely made me. I could see where this was going.

"I don't recall. In any case, welcome. We're so pleased your son, ..."

"Manuel," Mr. Lopez offered.

"Yes. We're so pleased Manuel applied to our fine institution."

I couldn't believe how nervous I was. For a moment, I felt like I was miscast in a play. I realized that the team was counting on my acting skills. My acting skills?

Certain something was off, Ms. Lopez looked at her husband and then the bodyguard. I reached for the drawer with my right hand. My left hand was on the desk underneath some of the papers.

"I have your son's file right here," I said as I started to open the drawer with my right hand.

"No!" Ms. Lopez commanded. She quickly retrieved a .38 caliber pistol from her purse and pointed it at me.

"Who hired you?"

She motioned for her bodyguard to move towards me. The thug walked toward me, pulling out a switchblade as he approached. I gripped the pistol I had hid underneath the papers. The barrel with silencer was conveniently pointed directly at Ms. Lopez.

"Who hired you?" she screamed.

I pretended I was going to say something and then squeezed the trigger, quickly firing two rounds. The first bullet hit Ms.

Lopez in the throat. The second glanced her left cheek as she slid down the chair. Didn't matter. The first shot was fatal.

Ms. Lopez reflexively fired a bullet into the floor before dropping the pistol and clutching her throat, blood spurting down her dress.

The bodyguard lunged at me as I started to aim the pistol at him. He tackled me before I could shoot.

The bodyguard knocked me back and we fell to the floor but I had a firm grip on the Glock. As we fell, I started to twist and squirm out from under the huge goon.

When we hit the floor, I had managed to end up on top. With the gun firmly grasped in my left hand, I fired. The first bullet hit the bodyguard underneath the jaw. It didn't stop him though.

Like a wounded rhino, the monster of a bodyguard leaned up which was a mistake. The next round caught him squarely in the face. His head slammed back on the floor with a sickening thud.

Rolling over I saw Senor Lopez opening the office door. I fired several rounds at him. A few hit the doorframe above and to the side of him. A few hit him in the back, causing him to fall forward.

I scrambled to my feet and ran to the door. Senor Lopez gasped for air as he crawled in a vain attempt to escape. I looked up to see Martha, gun drawn, run into the waiting area. She nonchalantly pumped two rounds into the cartel boss. He stopped moving.

"Let's go," Martha calmly said.

I followed her out of the office into a waiting black SUV, which sped off as soon as we hopped in. I didn't realize the bodyguard had slashed me until we were a few blocks off campus. Nothing too serious. Just thirty-six stitches down my left shoulder and bicep.

STAND DOWN

My Leon Black cover was supposed to be leveraged for potentially three jobs. The Ranier job, the Coles job and a job on one of the world's leading anarchists -- an outwardly bio-friendly, Portland-based organic farmer named Peter Ridgeway.

You know 'from farm to table.' In this case, it wasn't bright, beautiful unadulterated tomatoes being sold to environmentally conscious consumers but chaos. Violence. Looting. Breakdown of social order.

Underneath this innocent, even magnanimous façade, Ridgeway operated a global network of anarchist cells. He specialized in identifying conventional events where hyped-up crowds gathered for harmless reasons and co-oping the event for his deluded vision of a utopian society based on the collective without a state. That is, society without government.

Classic example being fans celebrating their sports teams winning championships. Or even losing as in the case of the Vancouver riots following their beloved Canucks losing the 2011 Stanley Cup Final.

Ridgeway would identify an event, develop a strategy and fund local cells to riot. Ridgeway had global lieutenants whom he would deploy to lead ground operations to ensure his simple yet powerful objective would be achieved - chaos. His ultimate objective was to release a biological agent that would in his words, 'reset world order and let evolution do its thing.'

On his 500-acre estate, Ridgeway had placed several 30-foot totem poles carved by a local artist - monuments to his heroes, including: Ted Kazinsky, the Unabomber; Franz Fanon, leader of the Algerian revolution which expelled the French imperialists; Jerry Mander, an early anti-technologist who was on Kazinsky's reading list; and the most recent one to none other than Ranier, which made me like this guy even less.

Did I mention Peter had a 500-acre estate? I'd have had more respect for the guy if he had worked hard to acquire the land but he 'earned it' the old fashion way – inheritance. In my opinion, Ridgeway was a spoiled brat who was bored.

Bored with hard work. Bored with building something sustainable. Bored with the status quo. Bored with the institutions that had been built over several generations by men and women who sacrificed for the greater good. Hope in a better future for the next generation.

Not our golden boy. Ridgeway thought he knew better. He saw oppression where others saw stability that helped local communities thrive. He saw stagnation where others saw security. Ridgeway saw boredom where others saw sustainability.

————————————

"We're on hold," Martha said.

"I'm fine. I have complete mobility," I said, rotating my shoulder.

"It's not my call. The folks at Langley are reviewing the medical report."

"Don't they know I'm terminal?" I asked facetiously.

Martha managed an almost imperceptible grin.

"Seriously, I want this one."

"Why?"

"Because he's smug."

"That's it?"

"Yes."

"OK. I expected a little more than that."

"He sits in his ivory tower without a worry in the world while he seeks destruction of social institutions that enable the average citizen to experience relative peace and security."

"Tell me how you really feel."

"I'm serious.

"Ridgeway's a joke. He doesn't even do his own research. Hell, at his pretentious dinner parties, he plagiarizes the Leon Black blog."

"So you've been listening to the surveillance tapes?" Martha genuinely laughed for the first time in my presence. I took it as a compliment but wasn't finished venting.

"This dickhead has the hubris to advocate transition to a stateless society? What do you tell the elderly and disabled during the destructive transition? No water. No food. Every man and woman for themselves. Sorry about that."

Martha nodded.

"If it wasn't so dangerous, it reminds me of that scene in Monty Python's Life of Brian where the anti-authoritarian Jews being parodied ask the question, 'what did the Romans ever do for us?'"

"That was funny," Martha said smiling. For what seemed like the first time, I noted that Martha had a nice smile.

"There's a reason why the Roman Empire endured for hundreds years. They provided basic services like sanitation."

Martha's mobile rang, interrupting my extended rant.

Martha answered, "Yes."

"OK." Martha hung up.

"Stand down is the order."

"Damn."

"I know."

I shook my head in disappointment.

"You're to report to Langley for a physical eval. Then you have a few personal days."

"What about Ridgeway?"

"Don't worry. He'll be dealt with."

"By who?"

"I'm not going to confirm whether there are other teams. You know I can't.

"Does it matter anyway?"

"Maybe."

"Maybe?"

"Yeah, maybe. I like the idea of an average Joe like me dealing with it.

"It just seems more special."

"Special?"

"I mean -- "

"Haven't you ever wondered? Are we the only country with this type of program?" Martha asked.

"Well, I suppose. We're basically where vigilantism collides with geopolitics."

"Yeah. State-sponsored vigilantism."

"So are you saying there are competing terminal agents? Like at the kidnappers at the cloud company?"

"I'm not saying anything."

"People like me. Men and women willing to die because they've been convinced they're dying."

"I'm just asking whether it's plausible for our enemies to use terminals to cause social unrest domestically - inciting racial violence for example."

"I guess anything is possible. I certainly never imagined I'd be a hit-man for the government."

"Yes, anything is possible."

PERSONAL INVENTORY

During my forced recuperation, in no particular order: I visited
Eileen, my mom and my best friend from high school; continued my
education regarding Japanese culture; got a positive health
update; and started practicing a card trick. You know, pick a
card, any card.

With respect to Eileen, I didn't actually visit with her. I went
to the home we used to share and saw her unloading groceries
with a guy whom I presumed was her new husband. I'd heard she
remarried.

I thought it was best to leave Eileen alone. She had made little
effort to stay in touch after our divorce, which was
understandable.

I harbored no ill will. Nor did I feel a connection. Kind of
like the girlfriend in college who said when she broke up with
me that it would have been different if I'd only joined a
particular fraternity. Good person. Just not on the same page.
No point in arguing about it. Forcing it to 'work.' Just let her
be. Eileen seemed happy and I was happy for her.

Visiting my mom was different. I had to see her one more time.
Hold her tight. Smile at her. Listen to her lyrical voice as she
described her various volunteer activities through the church
and local community. And if I was lucky, perhaps the smell fresh
banana bread would greet me.

I pulled up to my mom's two-bedroom rambler. Nothing special.
Her compact car was in the carport. Yard looked good but she
clearly hadn't spent any of the money I gave her from the sale
of all of my possessions.

As I got out of the car, I thought of all the hard times my mom
had faced. Was I a bad son for not staying to help? While I
believe the Agency manipulated my test results, I didn't know

54

for sure and I certainly didn't know 18 months ago. Regardless, I didn't want to burden my mom in case I was wrong. She didn't need to watch me decline.

She'd lost her parents at a young age and since my dad committed suicide, I didn't want to add more suffering to her life. She had always been stoic and I admired that. Maybe part of me didn't want to do anything that would dent my image of her: a heroic survivor; kind and loving; humble and strong.

―――――――――――

I knocked on the door. A few moments later, my mom opened the door and smiled at me.

"Oh my gosh. Why didn't you call?"

"I wanted to surprise you."

"Well you have. Come in.

"Come in sweetheart."

I came in and she hugged me tight. She closed the door. The small living room remained neat and tidy. Somewhat Spartan but decorated with things that mattered to my mom. Pictures of me, pictures of her and me and various religious figurines.

"How are you, Ben?"

I hadn't heard my real name for so long it almost didn't sound familiar.

"I'm good. How are you?"

"Oh, I'm fine. Keeping busy with the church and the women's guild.

"Let's sit."

"OK."

She sat on the couch and I sat in an armchair near her.

"That's great. I'm glad you're keeping busy, mom."

"In fact, I was thinking about you the other day when I was at Bible study. Wondering where you were and how you were."

"Don't worry about me mom. I'm fine."

"I know. I pray for you everyday."

"Thanks mom."

"But I thought of how difficult it was for you to lose your father just as you were becoming a man and I wondered whether that had anything to do with you and Eileen."

"Mom — "

"And I wondered whether I had failed you." Her voice cracked. I got up and sat next to her on the corduroy couch. I put my arm around her.

"Mom, don't say that. You've always been a great mother."

She retrieved a handkerchief from the side table and wiped her eyes and nose.

"I love you mom and I'm sorry I haven't stayed in touch more."

I wanted to tell mom what I was doing. That I was protecting her and her friends. Innocent children.

I wanted her to be proud of me. Check that. I know she was always proud of me but this was different. I believed I was really making a difference and not being able to share that with my mom hurt. But as the Stones song goes, we can't always get what we want.

Now composed, she said, "It's OK. I know your busy and doing important things at work.

"It's just that as you get older you sometimes look back and —"

"Mom, don't —"

"I just hope I've given you an anchor. Your father didn't have one and —"

"I know —"

"Anyway, in Bible study, we read a passage I hadn't read before. It's from the Old Testament. Maccabees."

"Uh, huh."

"Can I read it to you?"

"Sure."

She got up and went to the kitchen, returning with her well-used Bible.

"Here it is. 2 Maccabees verses 20 through 30. It's about a Hebrew mother and her seven sons. The king is trying to get them to renounce their faith by eating unclean food. Food offered to idols. He tries everything. Torture. Bribery. But the mother encourages her sons to hold firm."

I nodded as she started to read the passage.

"But the mother was especially admirable and worthy of honourable remembrance, for she watched the death of seven sons in the course of a single day, and bravely endured it because of her hopes in the Lord."

"The mother had already seen six of her seven sons killed," mom noted. I nodded.

"[21] Indeed she encouraged each of them in their ancestral tongue; filled with noble conviction, saying to them,

"[22] 'I do not know how you appeared in my womb,'" her voice cracked but she continued.

"'It was not I who endowed you with breath and life, I had not the shaping of your every part.

"[23] And hence, the Creator of the world, who made everyone and ordained the origin of all things, will in his mercy give you back breath and life, since for the sake of his laws you have no concern for yourselves.'"

"[24] Antiochus —"

"Antiochus was the King," mom said.

"Antiochus thought he was being ridiculed, suspecting insult in the tone of her voice; and as the youngest was still alive he appealed to him not with mere words but with promises on oath to make him both rich and happy if he would abandon the traditions of his ancestors; he would make him his friend and entrust him with public office.

"[25] The young **man** took no notice at all, and so the king then appealed to the mother, urging her to advise the youth to save his life.

"[26] After a great deal of urging on his part she agreed to try persuasion on her son.

"[27] Bending over him, she fooled the cruel tyrant with these words, uttered in their ancestral tongue, 'My son, have pity on me; I carried you nine months in my womb and suckled you three years, fed you and reared you to the age you are now, and provided for you.

"[28] 'I implore you, my child – '" My mom started to sob.

"Mom, you don't have to finish."

I squeezed her tight. She handed me the Bible to finish the reading. I started read.

"... look at the earth and sky and everything in them, and consider how God made them out of what did not exist, and that human beings come into being in the same way.

"[29] 'Do not fear this executioner, but prove yourself worthy of your brothers and accept death, so that I may receive you back with them in the day of mercy.'

"[30] She had hardly finished, when the young **man** said, 'What are you all waiting for? I will not comply with the king's ordinance; I obey the ordinance of the Law given to our ancestors through Moses.'"

I read, "The king had the young man killed."

We sat in silence. I stared at the burber carpet.

"I hope you know that you're loved by God more than I could ever love you."

"Yes," I replied.

"Isn't that amazing?"

"Yes. It is."

"When you left for college it hurt so bad my heart ached. Then I realized how much it must have pained God to send his Son Jesus when He knew Jesus would suffer terribly. That's when I realized how much I'm loved. And how much we're all loved."

My voice cracked, "I love you mom. Thanks for sharing that."

She pulled back and smiled at me before squeezing me tight. I didn't want to let her go. It was like I was five years old again with a scraped knee and she was comforting me.

I hoped she knew how much I loved her. How grateful I was for her.

Then I heard my voice reflexively say, "Well, I'd better go. My flight leaves in a few hours."

"OK. Do you want to take some chocolate chip cookies with you?"

"Do I?"

She smiled and went to the kitchen to get the cookies. As I looked around the small living room, I realized it isn't our possessions that make us wealthy but the love we share and my mom had shared a lot. I loved her and was proud of her.

We said our goodbye and I left. I wondered if I'd ever see her again. She assured me she didn't need any money. I believed her but took comfort that I had a $500,000 policy if I died, which was a much higher probabilty since switching 'careers' and of course, my 'diagnosis.'

I got in the rental car, waived and smiled as I drove away. Once out of sight, I broke down. I sobbed for lost time. Lost innocence. Choices long past. But mostly I sobbed in gratitude for my mom.

I had one more stop before leaving my hometown. I wanted to check in with my best friend from high school, Charlie. We had shared some great memories: sports highs and lows, girls highs and lows, general messing around and having fun. Basically, growing up. We went our separate ways in college, me going to the East Coast and Charlie stayed in the mid-west, but Charlie had been there for me when my dad took his life.

He had a basic wisdom and confidence that I always admired. We hadn't spent much time together in the past several years but had always managed to catch up once every year or so.

At the end of the end of the day though, Charlie knew me like few knew me. We had a history and a knowledge of each other that had been learned through victories, defeats, trials and celebrations. We shared many laughs and many tears.

We agreed to meet at a sports bar on my way out of town.

I arrived early. Pulled up a seat at the bar. It was March Madness so all of the TVs played a college hoops game.

Charlie walked in. He was a little heavier but still in good shape since I last saw him.

Charlie was the best athlete I had ever personally known. One of the few guys I knew who women hit on. Tall, dark, handsome and brooding.

I got up from my seat to greet Charlie. Shook hands and hugged.

"Great to see you, man," I said.

"Yeah, man."

Charlie pulled up a bar stool and I ordered a Bud for him.

"You remember. How thoughtful."

"Oh yeah. You're lucky I didn't order a shot of Tequila."

"Oh, no. Those days are long gone."

"Tell me about it."

We settled in. "So how are you, Ben?"

Again, I had heard my real name so infrequently it sounded strange.

"I'm good. How are you?"

"Good. Lindsay and the kids are well."

"That's great. How old are they now?"

"Kevin is 15, Grace 13 and Will is 11."

"All good athletes like their father?"

"Of course. Actually, Grace reminds me of you."

I laughed. "Oh really? Petite? Delicate?"

"No. I'm serious. She reads the play better than the boys and has great instincts. My only advice to her before a game is to trust her instincts and be aggressive."

"Cool."

The conversation dissipated. We stared at the TV screens above the bar.

"I miss you, Ben."

"I miss you too."

"How are you? Haven't heard as much from you since you and Eileen split."

"I know. I'm sorry."

"And you quit your job? What's up with that?"

I forgot. The Agency had me tell everyone I was taking an extended leave of absence. Told them I was on world tour. Sent post-cards to keep up the façade. No one at work questioned my story. Ultimately they moved on. As if I was never there.

I didn't have the energy to keep up the act.

"I wish I could tell you. I think you'd be proud but I can't."

"I believe you. And I am proud of you. Always have been."

I teared up. Charlie patted me on the shoulder.

"I wish we were kids again," he said.

"Mowing lawns, screwing around, playing hoops."

I had a hard time composing myself.

Charlie gave me a few moments.

Finally, I was able to say, "I sure miss you."

"Me too."

"And I'm happy for you. Lindsay's great and you're blessed with such great kids."

"Thanks. Means a lot coming from you."

I nodded.

"I'm worried about you but somehow know you'll be OK," Charlie said.

"Thanks. I think so too."

"Remember that Tecumseh poem?" Charlie asked.

"Yeah. Sort of."

"Something like, 'when it comes your time to die, be not like those whose lives are filled with the fear of death, so that when time comes they weep and pray for a little more time to live their lives over again in a different way. Sing your death song and die like a hero going home.' "

"Wow. Good memory," I said.

"I hope we've lived our lives somewhat like that."

"Me too."

I thought about it for a moment.

"You've done that, you know," I said.

"You've been a leader your entire life.

"You helped me at many critical times in my life and now you and Lindsay are raising three wonderful children, who will grow into leaders."

"I appreciate that," Charlie said.

After a few moments, Charlie asked, "How come you and Eileen never had kids?"

"Eileen didn't want kids and ... well after my dad, I didn't want to force it."

Charlie nodded.

"I didn't want to screw up any children."

"You'd have been a good dad, Ben."

"Thanks."

We sat in silence for a while. I broke the silence.

"Sorry but I need to head out."

"Yeah. Need to get up early tomorrow for a soccer tournament. Never ends, man."

I smiled. "I'm sure. Have a good time."

We got up. I paid the bill. Charlie offered but I insisted.

We exited the restaurant.

Outside we said our goodbyes.

"I stop by and see your mom every so often," Charlie said.

"She told me that. Can't tell you how much that means to me."

"No sweat. She's such a great lady. Always has chocolate-chip cookies and milk. Like when we were kids."

I smiled. "Yeah."

"I'll keep checking in on her every now and then."

"Thanks. I appreciate it."

"Take care, man."

"You too."

We got in our cars and Charlie drove away. I broke down again. I did have a great childhood. I was so grateful for growing up in middle America and having so much love in my life. My mom. Charlie.

As I pulled out of the lot, I was even more determined to progress in the program. Protecting Charlie and his family gave me additional motivation.

BACK ON THE HORSE

I didn't count killing the kidnapper as a job. Wasn't part of
the script. More of an improvisation so the cartel boss and his
wicked wife were jobs 2 and 3. Plus both Martha and I had kill
shots on the second kidnapper so it would be a stretch for me to
take full credit for that job.

While they say be careful what you wish for, truth be told, I
preferred the shootout required to free the CEO versus the
assassination style of my other jobs. Popping unsuspecting bad
folks, even if there were bad folks, didn't seem very sporting –
although the Fist Full of Dollars gunfight with the Mexican drug
trio was a little too close for comfort.

Regardless, as soon as my stitches were removed expectations
escalated quickly. The Agency needed a gut check. So did I.
Eliminating Colonel Coles was a now or never moment. Graduate or
be left behind.

The Agency couldn't continue its investment unless I could kill
a high-value target. After Oklahoma City, domestic terrorism was
a high priority for the feds. And Colonel Coles was near the top
of that list.

Of course, domestic matters were the jurisdiction of the FBI.
While the Bureau stiffs would be jagged off at the Agency
killing an FBI suspect, they would ultimately back off. Anyway,
all of my targets to date had been 'domestic.' I didn't care.
I'd leave the turf wars to the Washington bureaucrats.

For me, I needed a challenge to gage my progress. Shooting Dax
was like kicking a beanbag. It was like riding the pine for a
Single A team in Wichita. While killing the cartel boss and his
depraved wife and their bodyguard was a step up, perhaps Double
A ball, I still needed to prove to myself that I belonged in The
Show. That I could face a major league pitcher in Yankee
stadium, bottom of the ninth.

Coles didn't want to meet at his compound, which was a relief. You'd have needed an army to take care of business on his compound. It was a heavily armed fortress.

I couldn't believe he really wanted to meet an Internet putz like me, a/k/a Leon Black. It just goes to show that everyone, even incredibly paranoid racist cult leaders, has personal weaknesses to be exploited.

In this case, it was basic vanity. Despite saying he didn't care what the world thought of him, the Colonel did indeed care about his reputation. In fact, he craved a high Q Score.

He was envious of Leon Black's legion of followers. All it took was for Leon to cite some old articles written by the Colonel during his days teaching at Quantico. Even though his current philosophy was nearly unrecognizable in the lines of his prose back then, he found the citations flattering.

Through a complex set of intermediaries, the Colonel arranged the meeting. Talk about taking the bait. The nerds I made fun of back at Langley deserved huge credit for the web they weaved.

The meet with Coles was set for a local coffee shop, Common Ground, on the west end of Main Street in Bozeman. The set up, however, was more complicated. I would likely be frisked so there had to be a way to get me a gun once inside. The plan was for Martha to order coffee from the counter while I asked for change. I'd simply reach in to her purse and retrieve a pistol. Turn and start shooting.

Of course, all well laid plans can be FUBR.

I pulled up in a vintage Ford Bronco unaccompanied. I arrived before the Colonel, which was the first thing wrong with the plan.

Martha was seated in the back when I entered. She sipped a cup of coffee and contemplated eating the blueberry muffin sitting on a plate in front of her. She was reading the Bozeman Daily Chronicle, trying to look like a local.

That was another aspect of the plan that worried me. Too many new faces in the coffee shop, which could change the vibe and be noticed by the Colonel and his men.

Two beatnik women were behind the counter wearing the stereotypical sundresses and Birkenstocks. I wondered whether they shaved their underarms but quickly got back to business. I ordered a grande cappuccino from the 1st hipster, who worked the register. I couldn't see the face of the barista but was assured they'd bring my cappuccino over when ready.

I took a seat in middle of the café, near a window that ran along an alleyway. A few minutes later, the cash register girl delivered my coffee. Ten minutes after that, a black Chevy Suburban pulled up. A former special-forces type exited the driver's side, walked in front of the SUV and opened the passenger door. The Colonel exited.

I could tell from the briefing photos and surveillance video. Short-cropped hair, pale weathered-complexion, toned upper body and ever present black Ray Bans.

Coles and his bodyguard entered the coffee shop as another member of his security detail hopped in the driver's side. He pulled the SUV into the alley and parallel parked alongside the coffee shop.

Once they entered, I discretely waived. The bodyguard approached and asked if I was Leon.

"Yes," I said as I stood up. The burly dude nodded for me to open my jacket. He frisked me as expected. He retrieved a snub nose .38 revolver from my waistband.

"Anything else?"

"No."

Surprisingly, he didn't frisk me further. Just nodded to Coles, who casually walked over. The Colonel removed his sunglasses.

"Mr. Black?"

"Yes, Colonel. Pleasure to meet you."

"Pleasure is mine. Please sit." We sat down.

"Do you want anything?"

"No. I'm fine."

The Colonel was confident. No starlight in his eyes. It caught me off guard. I expected to have the advantage. I was counting on a celebrity freeze but was wrong.

"You seem nervous Mr. Black."

"Well ... I'm an admirer ..."

"Really, give me some specifics."

"Well ..." The damn briefing better have been accurate.

"Well, for starters, I admired how you were one of the chief architects of the surge ... an attempt to regain some semblance of order in Iraq."

The Colonel nodded ever so slightly but I could tell he was flattered.

"Didn't matter. It's a mess over there."

"Sure is."

The Colonel flashed a look, indicating he wasn't looking for my view.

"Should have never invaded. Should have listened to the old guard."

I nodded, offering no commentary.

"Former head of NSA, even wrote a WSJ op-ed, trying to convince the Bush administration not to invade. Same rationale his father relied upon not to take down Bagdad."

I leaned in. Genuinely interested.

"Iraq kept Iran and Syria in check. Even kept the Kurdish problem in check, which stabilized Turkey.

"The Bush administration made an error of historical proportions. Unleashed chaos."

I nodded.

"Intentions were good but totally naïve.

"Even the fucking head of the CIA was naïve."

Mention of CIA caught me off guard. I hoped it didn't show.

"When the President asked what would happen after we removed Sadam, the Director said they'd welcome us as conquering heroes.

"Should have fired his ass."

The cash register girl came to the table. "Can I get you two cowboys anything?"

The Colonel shook his head while I said, "No thanks." The girl walked away.

I caught myself wondering what Martha was doing. I hoped she didn't go to the counter too soon. I hoped she noticed the Colonel was commanding my full attention.

"Should have fired him and told him he had four weeks to win his job back by outlining the worst case scenario and giving the President three options to deal with a worst case scenario.

"If none of those options were viable, should have never invaded."

I nodded.

"Anyway, me and my followers aren't naïve."

"How so?"

"I've talked enough. Tell me about your network. How you developed it. What your plans are to grow it. Maintain it."

"Well, I'm flattered you want to know." I looked at my coffee cup, which was nearly empty.

"Looks like I need a refill." I started to get up, "Can I get you one?"

The Colonel firmly grabbed my wrist.

"She'll come back. Let's focus on answering my questions."

Surprised, I said, "OK."

I sat back down. Another wildcard.

"Alright. OK. Where to start?"

'Shit,' I thought to myself. I hadn't planned on this.

Going from what I recalled from the briefing, I started.

"It's about leveraging existing platforms. You know. Facebook. Twitter."

Coles nodded.

"Linking with influential bloggers," I smiled.

Coles allowed himself a smile.

"Integration with platforms like Craigslist is key. And monitoring metrics, bounce rate, stickiness, etc. are critical to refine your efforts. Ultimately you want to create a viral loop."

Coles seemed genuinely interested. I almost forgot why I was there when I noticed Martha at the counter.

It was now late morning. The in-between time for a café. All of the patrons had left except for me, the Colonel, Martha and the Colonel's bodyguard.

Now how to break the conversation and get to the counter.

"I shouldn't have had a double shot. Need to use the restroom. Do you mind, Colonel?"

Coles seemed suspicious. I felt like Michael Corleone facing the Turk and the crooked Captain McCluskey in the Bronx restaurant.

After an uncomfortable silence, Coles said, "Sure. It's a free country."

"Is it?" I joked. Fell flat. The Colonel didn't break a smile.

I got up and glanced at the counter. Martha was stalling but I had to go through the pretense of visiting the toilet otherwise the Colonel and his crew would certainly know something was afoot.

I moved quickly but not too quickly. I entered the narrow bathroom and started to wait for what I thought would be an appropriate time. Fact was I couldn't have produced any juice if I wanted to. I was more nervous for this job than any other for some reason. Maybe it was my close interaction with the target.

Anyway, my anxiety was interrupted by the sound of a gunshot.

I rushed out of the bathroom to see the Colonel's bodyguard on top of Martha, choking her. I grabbed a knife from a nearby table and lunged at the bodyguard. I buried the knife in the guy's neck and pulled him off Martha in one motion. Martha quickly scrambled to her feet in pursuit of the Colonel.

As I rolled over, I looked up to see the barista holding a 9mm Beretta. She expertly fired bullets through the café window. I leaned up and saw the barista chick's shots hit the Colonel, who slumped against the SUV. The driver had exited the car and fired back. The barista was hit by a few bullets and fell hard to the floor.

I crawled over to her and checked her pulse. The barista was alive but badly wounded. I looked out the window to see Martha pump the driver with slugs as he tried to load the Colonel into the vehicle. As I held the barista in my arms, I looked closely at her. She was wearing a red wig that was now eschew. She looked familiar. Her green eyes. Fresh complexion.

It was Tracy. I felt sick. Sinead O'Connor's surreal dirge-like of <u>Foggy Dew</u> played in the background, hanging like a pall.

The extraction team arrived in two separate vans. I cried, "Help her."

The team hastily scooped Tracy from my arms and took her to the first van. Other team members then led me out of the café into the second van. Martha was inside.

The van door slid closed and the two vehicles sped away.

"That was Tracy," I said.

"I know."

"Why didn't you tell me?"

"I couldn't risk breaking her cover."

"Bullshit."

"I know you're pissed. I don't blame you."

"Shit." I leaned forward and ran my hands through my hair without realizing they were covered in Tracy's blood.

"She's hurt bad."

"I'm sorry."

"Me too." My voice cracked. Martha reached out for my hand. I angrily pulled it back.

THE DEVIL'S BANKER

I was worried about Tracy. The Agency wouldn't give me any
information, which made me furious. I hoped and prayed she was
OK.

I just wanted her to be safe. Tracy was incredibly intelligent,
energetic and charismatic. She would have been a great
businesswoman. An artist. Whatever she set her mind to. But
somehow I doubted that was her fate. The Agency got its hooks
into her so young.

To distract my mind, I threw myself further into preparing for
Ranier but kept getting presented with other 'opportunities.' I
know it sounds weird, possibly pathological and even arrogant
but some jobs seemed mundane, even pedestrian while others, no
pun intended, were killer assignments.

I have to admit I wasn't sure if the Agency simply viewed me as
a nutcase who would take any assignment regardless of how
reckless or whether the Agency believed I was the best choice
for a particular job. You know, like your crazy college buddy
who'd holds a bottle rocket above his head at the party until it
explodes - except in this case the risk is death instead of a
sore hand. Or was I a respected, even valuable asset. I didn't
like to believe I was dispensable but knew I was deluding myself
on some level.

Whatever the case, in addition to the whacking the leaker, I was
pumped about one particular opportunity - the elimination of a
London banker who helped the evil monster, ISIS, launder their
illicit funds.

I realized it would only be a minor dent in a increasingly
potent vehicle of death and destruction but the way I looked at
it - taking out a facilitator like Ahmed El Eran, the devil's
banker, would send a message to those who commit sins of
omission not just sins of commission. You know, like in
Unforgiven when Clint's Will Money tells the dime-store author
to pick up a gun, if you're going to help finance a war, you'd
better carry a weapon.

So when Martha presented the El Eran job, I didn't hesitate. Plus this job would require the use of a blunt instrument as opposed to the Ranier job, which would require finesse and nuance. By that, I mean I was going to shoot this fucker in the face. This one would let me express my anger over Tracy and at an amorphous band of psychos who harkened to the medieval era. You know, beheadings, slavery, monument destruction.

The fact our own esteemed leader, when commenting on ISIS, felt compelled to remind the Western world of the Crusades massively missed the point, and frankly insulted the brave men and women protecting our country and amounted to spitting on the graves of innocent victims. You don't read headlines today about Christians beheading non-Christians or selling captives as sex slaves or blowing up priceless artifacts. Where is the outrage? Not sure if our esteemed leader was a sheep, chief enforcer of political correctness run amok, or whether he saw the situation as payback for the Western world's past sins. Either way, I said screw him. Sign me up.

"The set up is straight forward," Martha said.

"Every morning without exception at approximately 08.00, on his way his office on Pall Mall, El Eran stops for a smoke in St. James Square in London's West End. He leisurely strolls through the park and drags on his cigs, periodically checking his handheld."

"While his client rains death and destruction on whoever opposed its perverse view of the world," I added.

"Yes. Basically."

Martha still never engaged in banter with me. On the one hand, she was an ice queen; on the other hand, she was calm, cool and collected, which I respected.

"We'll drop you off at Trafalgar Square where you'll get a black cab to the square at half seven."

I nodded.

"You meander along the perimeter until El Eran arrives."

"Then I enter the park where I close in and pop him. Double-tap to ensure he won't process any more deposits or withdrawals for his evil client."

"Yep. And then make your way back to the safe house in Marylebone. I'll meet you there and we'll make our way to London City Airport. One of the Agency's jets will whisk us back to the US."

"Roger that."

Martha raised an eyebrow.

"Let's review the photos again. These are from earlier this week. Very fresh."

I studied the photos. El Eran's eyes were cold and black as coal. His background was sketchy but thought to be of Egyptian descent. Educated in the UK. Briefing was inconclusive whether he was a true believer or a greedy bastard who didn't care what his clients did with their money.

My summation, "He looks like he could behead someone."

"How would you know? And isn't that convenient stereotyping?"

"Which question do you want me to answer first?"

"Don't answer either. You've made yourself clear."

"Fine. I'm not going to apologize for what we're going to do. Are you?"

"Just review the photos one more time."

At the appointed hour, Martha and the insertion team dropped me at Trafalgar Square. Martha mustered up, "Good luck."

"Thanks," I said as I exited a sleek silver van. Then I flagged down one of the famous London black cabs. It was a stereotypical grey, drizzly English day. As the cab navigated through the quaint but discombobulated streets of London, I found myself looking forward to this job more than any other so far.

Truth be told, for the other jobs so far, I was anxious and curious more than motivated. This time, I was excited. It was like playing against your archrival – except this game was for all the marbles.

I momentarily reflected how much I had changed during 20 months in the program. I wondered how I'd come to feel excited about killing a man. Life as an anonymous, average Joe seemed like a lifetime ago. I also realized that the program worked.

Whether I was dying or the Agency convinced me I was dying, the Agency's gamble paid off. I was willing to die because I'd been convinced I was dying.

Was it my father's suicide that drove me on? He just quit. Gave up. No fight. I wasn't going to quit. Losing all of our family's money had driven me to join the SEC. Now I wondered whether the ghost of my father's failure was again chasing me.

———————————

The cab turned off of Pall Mall onto Waterloo Place past a statute to British soldiers who had fought in the Crimean War. A war I had never heard of before. One that found the British, the French and the Ottoman Empire aligned against Russia. Seemed weird that almost 200 years later, Crimea would take center stage on the geopolitical landscape – marking Russia's reassertion of its pre-Cold War territorial perspective. Whatever you think about Putin, at least he isn't a sheep. Certainly not a sheepdog. More of a wolf but definitely not a sheep.

In fact, there were rumors Putin periodically vanquished domestic enemies with his own hand, not relying surrogates to do the dirty work. Putin, the theory went, committed these acts so that when he negotiated with other world leaders, he knew he was capable of going balls to the wall compared to 99% of the think-tank plutocrats posing as strategic, global leaders. Putin felt it gave him an invaluable edge. Dark and sinister but you could see his twisted rationale.

The black cab turned left onto Charles II Street. St. James Square was straight ahead. St. James used to be a high-end residential area of London but over time had become more of a commercial area, home to the head offices for multinational giants like British Petroleum and Rio Tinto. I asked the cab driver to pull over. I paid and exited the cab at approximately 7.30 a.m.

I entered the square through one of the four entrances, one on each of the park's four sides. The square was surrounded a black, rod iron fence. Inside the park there was a paved circular path with crisscross paths cutting through the park and a statue of William III in the center. William the Third was famous for inventing the pancake.

I'm joking. I skipped most of my Western Civ classes in college so who knows what the guy did. Anyway, the rest of the park was well-groomed grass patches and abundantly populated flowerbeds.

I exited the park on the opposite side and slowly walked around the perimeter, waiting for El Eran to show up. Did I have any doubts about the briefing? Was I being misled like Job #1? No. The briefing had been thorough.

The evidence against the bank was substantial. The Brits and the US would be indicting the bank's principals within days, shutting the bank down and seizing its assets and its clients' assets. But the Agency and perhaps others wanted to send a message. If you aid and abet the enemy, you'll pay. I was happy to deliver the invoice.

El Eran arrived on cue. He wore a light, tan raincoat. He casually walked around the outer path within the square as he puffed on a cigarette.

I didn't waste time. I entered the park and walked directly toward him at a normal pace. As I approached about 20 yards away, El Eran nonchalantly reached in the right pocket of his

©2014
Jake Weidman

overcoat. He pulled out a pistol, pointed it at me and fired. What the fuck?

As I said, be careful for what you wish for. Maybe the Agency didn't value me as much as I hoped. I dove to my right behind a park bench. I heard the splinter of wood as one or two bullets hit the bench. I rolled to my right into one of the flowerbeds.

El Eran stopped firing. I drew my gun as I rose to a crouched position. I scanned the park to see El Eran running out of the park and up Duke of York Street.

I popped up and chased after him. As I exited the park, El Eran was half way up Duke of York Street, which was under construction. A dump partially blocked the street, which slowed him down.

As I closed in, El Eran turned left on Jermyn Street. About 100 yards up the street, he cut right into one of the quaint shopping arcades in London, the Princess Street Arcade. Based on the briefing, I knew that Piccadilly Street was on the other end of the alleyway and I didn't want him to make it to the typically busy pedestrian area even though it was early morning.

As I approached the arcade, a bullet shattered the glass of a men's hat shop on the corner. I slipped and fell hard to the ground as shards of glass rained down. I skidded to an abrupt stop. El Eran had stopped mid-way through the arcade. He was leaning in the doorway of a candy shop on the left hand side.

I scooted and rolled to my left until I was safely behind cover. Breathing heavily, adrenalin pumping, I realized this guy was kicking my ass. Making me look bad. And I got angry. El Eran wasn't going to get to the other end of the arcade. If I waited any longer, he'd takeoff so I got up and started to run down the arcade tunnel.

El Eran peaked out from behind the candy shop entryway and saw me coming. He looked surprised but fired a few more bullets at me. I dove forward to the ground and as I did I fired multiple rounds at him. I saw the first bullet hit him in the torso and the next few shattered glass around him. He stumbled forward and

I fired a few more bullets into him as he crumpled face-first to the ground.

I rose to my feet and walked over to him. He was still breathing but hurt badly. Probably mortally wounded.

I kicked him to roll him over. He looked at me with extreme prejudice, which I certainly understood. It was mutual. El Eran futility raised his hand to try to fire one more bullet at me. I stepped on his hand, pinning it and his gun, a Russian 9x18mm Makarov, to the ground.

I fired one in his head for insurance. I didn't feel any sympathy. This asshole and his comrades had viciously and without remorse killed thousands of innocents and driven millions more from their homes. For all the suffering associated with the European refugee situation, imagine how bad things were for people to risk life and limb to leave their homes for an uncertain future.

Bottom line, they were driven from their homes by murderous lunatics and El Eran was just one of many who needed to be brought to justice. I walked away confident I'd won a victory, albeit small, for the good guys.

I put my pistol back in its holster, dusted myself off and walked up the arcade to Piccadilly Street. Once on Piccadilly, I found the first bus stop and caught the next bus. I rode one of the iconic red double-decker buses a few blocks and exited near Green Park. I then caught a taxi to Marylebone High Street. The safe house was a few blocks from there.

What the F?

Inside the safe house, a sparsely decorated one-bedroom apartment, Martha and I informally debriefed while we waited for transport to London City Airport.

"Are you OK?"

I shook my head. "Yeah. I guess so."

We anxiously paced back and forth, trying not to bump into one another. Tracy and I would have 'celebrated' no matter how little time we had. Of course, things were different with Martha.

Anyway, I was pissed.

"What the hell?"

"I know. It was as if he was expecting you."

"Really?"

I sounded suspicious.

"It must be some sort of fluke. There's no way he could have been tipped. He must have been hyper paranoid."

"I know the feeling."

Martha was silent. She stopped pacing and turned her back to me. She made a strange noise. I was annoyed. I grabbed her shoulder and spun her around.

Surprisingly, the noise I heard her make was laughter. Martha started laughing harder than I'd ever heard her laugh, which irritated the shit out of me under the circumstances.

"I'm sorry," Martha said, barely able to compose herself.

"What?!"

She shook her head. "You slipped pretty badly."

I was confused momentarily then remembered my ungraceful entrance into the arcade. As I recalled the scene, I started to laugh too -- a combination of anxious relief and genuine humor.

"I guess it was comical."

"I'm sorry. It's just that -"

"Wait! How did you know?"

"We were following you almost real time. London has one of the most sophisticated networks of surveillance cameras in the world. You know, CCTV on every corner."

"But how --?"

"We hacked in."

I nodded.

"Can I see?"

Martha hesitated then said yes.

"Go wipe your forehead first. You have a bruise and some blood."

"No wonder the taxi driver and everyone on the bus was staring at me. I thought they knew what happened."

"Speaking of paranoid."

"Yeah. I know," I said as I walked into the tiny bathroom to clean up.

After I cleaned up, I joined Martha at a basic white table in the dining area of the apartment. I pulled up a chair and sat next to Martha as she cued the video.

The video followed me from exiting the taxi at St. James Square to me running out of the park to chasing El Eran to me slipping to the ground at the arcade. Martha giggled at my clumsiness and I laughed as well. My ex-father-in-law used to say 'you have to be able to laugh at yourself.'

I was leaning in close to the video. There was a noise outside. When Martha turned toward the window, she and I bumped heads. We smiled at each other. Locked in on each other's eyes and by some strange force we moved closer to each other until our lips touched.

Soft. Tender. Kiss.

Martha's mobile, which was sitting on the table, lit up and vibrated -- interrupting the moment.

Martha pulled back, "I'm sorry."

In that brief moment, I felt at home. It had been a long-time since I felt at home.

"Yeah," I muttered.

She answered the call. Listened and said, "OK. Be down in two."

"They're here." Transport had arrived.

As we gathered our things, I asked, "Can I see other videos? You know, for training purposes?"

I was also curious to see myself in action, hoping I looked cool. Kind of like breaking down film after a victory.

Martha hesitated then said, "Sure."

"Great."

Martha stopped and looked at me.

"What?"

"You know, you're the star of the shows?"

"What do you mean?"

"I mean, the tapes have all be edited so that you're the only Agency asset who appears."

"Hmm."

"Yes, hmm."

"What am I missing?"

"If you're ever caught, your on your own. The Agency will deny your existence."

"I guess I'm not surprised. Should I be?"

"Maybe not but I thought you should know."

So I was on my own? On the one hand sad. On the other hand, liberating.

"What about the university job?"

"Just a crazed admissions officer on a rampage."

"What about you ... coming in at the end?"

"Just you.

"Of course, CIA, through various federal surrogate agencies, would first seek to tie up any public disclosures under national security gag orders.

"But if the Agency ever had to produce video footage or show it to officials in an off-the-record briefing, all you would see is you shooting Lopez as he futilely crawled across the carpet."

I nodded. "Thanks for telling me."

"And the Agency will have a dossier of your lone wolf activities. Bank trail. Online trail. Travel logs. Everything to tie off your connection with the powers that be."

"So I'm stuck? I'm dispensable if I stop or became ineffective."

Martha was silent.

"I'm a valued asset as long as I'm producing. Like an NFL running back. Short shelf life."

"Like you always say, no loose ends."

"Yeah. No loose ends."

We exited the safe house.

MARTHA — MY TURANDOT

As we prepared for the ultimate job, the job I presumed I, and others like me were recruited to complete, Martha educated me on opera. Ranier loved opera and I had to be well versed enough to carry on a conversation as the Leon Black blog would make periodic operatic references. One of several threads the Agency hoped would lure Ranier in for a meet.

––––––––––––––––––––––

"Opera is simply an art form combining poetry, dance and music where the singers and musicians perform a drama," Martha said. "The drama is a combination of the libretto or words and the musical score."

"First opera was performed in Florence, Italy in 1598," I responded.

"Yes. And the name of the opera performed?"

"Dafne?"

"Yes. Opera spread from Italy to Germany, France and then England in the 17th century."

"What does the word 'opera' mean in Italian?"

"Means work."

"Yes. And 'libretto'?"

"Literally, it means 'small book' but it refers to the words of an opera. The story."

"Good. Some composers wrote there own libretti while others worked with librettists."

"Kind of like us," I said.

"Yeah. I guess so."

While Martha contemplated my comment further, I recalled sitting on the same back porch at the Agency safe house in rural

Virginia. The same porch where I got to know more about Tracy as a person on a crisp fall day.

This particular day was an indecisive spring day. You know the kind where it's tempting to wear flip-flops and shorts only to regret it later.

While I missed Tracy and still didn't know whether she was OK, I enjoyed working with Martha. It seemed more professional. I'd be lying to say that the sex with Tracy wasn't awesome but I'd also be lying if I denied that the Agency had used the sex to manipulate me early on in the program.

I still didn't understand why Tracy would let herself be used. Maybe the Agency had something on her. Or maybe her 'condition' created a win-win situation that the Agency exploited.

During my time with Tracy, the jobs were blunt. Bang, bang. Over. Like sex with Tracy.

It was different with Martha. No sex. Just the possibility of it. Other than the brief kiss we shared in London we had no intimate contact.

I glanced over at Martha. She was reading from the briefing. She wore black jeans, a teal sweater and white socks. No shoes.

It really didn't matter what Martha wore. Clothes didn't adorn her. She made them better.

"What's your favorite aria?" Martha asked.

""Au fond du temple saint" from Georges Bizet's <u>The Pearl Fishers</u>."

"Why?"

"Reminds me of my best friend in high school."

"That doesn't sound like Leon Black."

"OK. I like it because it reminds me of two best friends lamenting the oppression of the state. Facing death and desolation together."

86

"Good. That's more like it."

"How about something more upbeat?"

"An aria similar to "Libiamo, ne' lieti calici" from Verdi's <u>La Traviata</u>."

Martha nodded. "Good."

Martha looked out at the trees and the fading sunlight.

"Let's take a walk before it gets dark," I said.

Martha hesitated then said she'd get her shoes.

We walked side by side down a dusty trail in the woods. The safe house was not too far from Skyline Drive in the Shenandoah Valley about an hours drive from Washington DC. A series of bucolic rolling hills covered with deciduous trees, mainly oaks.

"Can I ask you something?"

"Sure," Martha said.

"Why did you join the Agency?"

"Well, it's complicated."

"I've got time."

We walked in silence for a bit.

"You know how I said only you appear in the surveillance tapes?"

"Yes. I'm a terminal so I'm expendable."

"Well, I lied. I'm in the tapes too."

"What?"

"Like the Lopez hits.

"I'm on tape shooting Senor Lopez as he crawls on the carpet."

"I don't understand."

"I'm in the program too. Have been for more than five years."

"Are you ill?"

"I don't think so."

"Were you ever ill?"

"I don't know. Just like you."

"So why are you in the program?"

"Probably same reason you are."

"I'm a believer. I think we're making the world safer."

"Yeah but -"

"Plus, I don't know how to stop," I interrupted.

"I know. Me neither."

"Have you seen anyone quit?"

"No. Some killed. Some disappeared. Maybe they resigned. I don't know."

"What about Tracy?"

"No. She was recruited out of college."

I nodded.

We walked along a bit further.

"We should turn back," Martha said.

"Yes."

As we turned around, Martha paused.

"I couldn't expose Tracy. I'm sorry."

"I know. Is she OK?"

"I don't know."

Martha looked into my eyes.

"About Montana."

I moved closer.

"Yes."

"I never thanked you for saving my life."

"You'd have done the same for me."

Martha nodded. I reached out and pulled her to me.

We embraced and kissed. A long passionate kiss.

A chilly breeze blew through the trees, causing us to hold each other even tighter and kiss even deeper.

OH, IT'S ON

I have to give the Agency geeks some serious props. They weave elaborate webs, exploiting the virtues, vices and vanities of targets to slowly but steadily pull them in. Coles was one such example.

Ranier was even more paranoid. Highly skittish. Like the elusive bonefish. He was simultaneously in hibernation and had finely tuned senses.

Nonetheless, the Leon Black blog did the trick. A steady stream of libertarian diatribe, well-researched arguments, disregard for personal fame and no public appearances. Professed admiration for Ranier. The vanity play.

The Langley techies also established essential off-the-grid credentials for the fictitious Leon Black. Ranier presumably had time on his hands, which also helped.

The first contact was on a Saturday night, approximately 22:00 local time in Russia. Through highly encrypted pipes, Ranier pinged Leon Black. Message was simple: "Do you want to chat? A fan."

Now under any other circumstances, one would probably ignore such an innocuous question. But the Agency had hundreds of people on the case, who had time to follow up on any and all such requests. That's how CIA reeled in Coles and Ridgeway.

The Agency arranged for a Skype session with Ranier. I was brought into Langley for the session. You can't imagine what kind of resources went into the preparation. Like a Mars landing.

The Agency followed the encryption protocol sent by Ranier. The Agency geeks were both impressed by the protocols and disturbed. Whatever the geeks thought of Ranier's actions, they were clearly awed by his skills.

No expense was spared. I even shaved my goatee.

No less than three tele-prompters were made available to me,
pre-loaded with answers to questions Ranier may ask. Each
monitored by three IT folks who could search for relevant
content in response to questions, quickly feeding me with
answers to maintain credibility.

We held five practice sessions. Each session was four hours and
the prep team put on me as much pressure as possible.

At first, I suspected the Agency was vetting at least two or
three agents for the Ranier interaction. But then I sensed the
tone change from vetting to helping me prepare for the real
session.

The Bright Lights

The Skype session with Ranier consisted of a series of rapid-fire questions posed by Ranier regarding Japanese culture, check; and current events, check. Ranier didn't appear on screen for most of the 'interview.'

I responded as best I could. The pace actually helped me focus and forget how staged the whole event was on our end.

I was located in a conference room inside the bowels of Langley with black felt blankets draped on all four sides, forming a 12' by 12' room of sorts. The teleprompters were fanned out behind the camera that filmed me.

Ranier finally appeared on screen. Looked like he was in a hotel.

"Where are you?" Ranier asked.

"Are you serious? Anyone who knows my blog knows remaining out of site is key to it success. That's how it works. That's how I've been able to stay alive and independent."

"Alive?" Ranier was skeptical.

"Yes. Alive. As my followers have grown so has the threat."

"Threat to who?"

"The establishment."

"Why'd you start the blog?"

I paused to genuinely contemplate. I hadn't really connected with the Leon Black character and that had sufficed so far. But now I sensed a do or die moment.

"There was a void that needed to be filled."

Silence. Did I pass the test?

After a long pause, Ranier said, "Tell me about yourself."

"I don't like talking about myself."

"I respect that."

I nodded then Ranier said, "You're probably less interesting in person but there's something I can only tell you in person."

Bait taken.

"OK. Do you want my address?"

Ranier laughed hard.

After composing himself and savoring the levity for a moment, Ranier said, "No. Let's meet here in Moscow. Do you like opera?"

That's the one topic he hadn't covered for some reason.

"Well ... " I paused, playing hard to get.

"What else do you have to do? Don't you want to meet your hero?"

"Is the Dali Lama going to be there?"

The briefing indicated Ranier loved spirited repartee. I was advised not to rollover or defer too much. Ranier respected dissent.

Said a lot about the man in my view. Kind of explained why Ranier did what he did. Not so much a selfless revolutionary like John Brown at Harper's Ferry but more of a Michael Moore pissing in the pool. Action for sake of reaction. Gleefully soaking up the attention as opposed to considering the consequences of one's actions.

Ranier laughed. I sighed in relief. Continue to trust the briefing I told myself.

"Sure," I relented.

"Great. Turadot is playing at the Kolobov Saturday the 12th."

"OK."

"Do you know Turadot?"

"Not seen it but I knew the story from Martha and my prep work – a prince falls in love with a cold princess. To obtain permission to marry the princess, her suitors have to solve three riddles or die."

"Yes. I like riddles."

"Not me," I said.

"So is it a date?"

"Yes. Look forward to it."

"One final thing," Ranier said.

"Yeah."

"Take the camera and sweep the room so I can see all sides."

A moment of panic.

"OK. Why?"

"Just humor me."

"OK. Let me get up."

I moved slowly. The technicians started to remove the tele-prompters. I started whistling to cover up any ambient noise.

"Why are you whistling?"

I pretended not to hear him.

He asked louder this time, "Why are you whistling?"

The technicians were almost done. "Why? Is it annoying?"

"Just scan the room." I didn't want to push it. I stopped whistling.

"Yep."

I pulled the camera from the tripod and scanned the room, starting from the back, then left, then right, and just as the technicians removed the final tele-prompter, the front.

"OK. See you soon."

"See you soon."

DRAW THE CURTAINS

The Kolobov Novaya Opera Theatre of Moscow was an iconic theatre remodeled in 1997 after the fall of the Soviet Union.

After entering the ornate theatre, I navigated my way to the ticket counter where I picked up a prearranged ticket. I had been instructed to wait there. Someone would meet me. I scanned the anteroom while waiting.

An odd assortment of people streamed into the venue. People who fit the classic pre-Glasnost Leonid Brezhnev stereotype – excessively bushy eyebrows, Neanderthal foreheads and bad teeth. But there was a healthy dose of Lincoln Center, Manhattan investment banker types and, of course, Middle Eastern sheiks and even the occasional nerdy American lawyer.

My nose itched. I carefully scratched it.

Two Klitschko-esque bodyguards in tailored suits interrupted my people watching. The two Goliaths led me to one of the boxes near the stage. The box was spacious with two high-back, green velvet chairs and an antique coffee table between the two chairs. Once inside the box, I waited for the bodyguards to indicate which chair I should sit in but they just glared at me. Irritated, I picked the chair on the right.

A program for the opera sat on each of the two seats in the box. I sat down and started to read the program, conveniently translated into English. The audience steadily streamed into the theatre. Ranier still hadn't shown up.

Meanwhile, the two bodyguards flanked the entrance to the box. The guards were either private security provided by media companies or Russian government. The Agency suspected the latter. Made sense to me. I never believed it was a happy coincidence that Ranier ended up in the former Soviet Union.

The first act started. The opera begins with a solitary figure announcing that, "Any man who desires to wed Turandot must first answer three riddles. If he fails, he will be beheaded."

'Glad Eileen's dad didn't have a similar test,' I thought.

Anyway, the Persian prince fails and is beheaded. Made me think of the banker hit with satisfaction.

I checked my watch. Was Ranier going to no-show me? Big-time me?

A crowd gathers where the Persian prince is killed. Imperial guards push the crowd back, including an old blind man. His assistant cries out and a young man, the Prince of Tartary, comes to their aid. When he does so, he recognizes the old man as his long-lost father – the deposed king of Tartary.

My mind wandered as I waited. I hoped he wouldn't want to talk about the gay Japanese anime. My nose itched but I resisted itching it.

Mid-way through the first act, Ranier made his entrance. Another two security guards arrived with him.

He brought a metal brief case, which held his own wine, wine glass and cheese. Not a surprise as the briefing had noted his extreme paranoia about the risk of being poisoned and therefore would bring his own food and drink. He nodded at me and took a seat.

He methodically opened the wine and cheese. He even had a sliced apple wrapped in a napkin. He giggled like a child when the cork popped.

He nibbled on the cheese and apples like a rat and annoyingly sipped a glass of sauvignon blanc throughout the remainder of the first act. I wanted to punch him in the face just for being so irritating.

At the end of Act 1 a large gong is struck three times. Ranier and everyone in the theatre intently looked at the stage. I took this as an opportunity to pick my nose. I know its childish but the Agency geniuses glued a small, clear Saran tablet inside my right nostril. I held it in my right hand.

The Agency assured me the poison wouldn't be absorbed into my system but only activated by the alkaline in the wine. I felt comfortable relying on their assurances for several reasons but mainly because they wanted me to kill Ranier and it was fast acting. They wouldn't want me to die before administering the fatal pill.

At the first intermission, the crowd shuffled out to visit the bathroom or get a drink. Several no doubt to go for a smoke.

_____

Ranier broke the ice. "How do you like the opera?"

"It's OK. Amazing soprano but I prefer the libretto from Verdi's La Traviata."

"I find Verdi's libretto in La Traviata's a pretentious diatribe," Ranier countered.

"Takes one to know one," I said. Remember, Ranier liked dissension. It defined his worldview.

Ranier snickered, "Touché."

I took no satisfaction that I was playing him but continued to play the part. "Don't get me wrong. I know what you mean." He nodded.

Seeing Ranier in person was different than I expected. He was 28 years old when he made his fateful decision. Now 30 years old, he looked much older. His sandy brown hair was prematurely greying. His eyes had wrinkles too deep for someone his age and the dark bags under his eyes begged the question of whether he was really at peace with his actions. Either way, his eyes revealed an unsettled mind.

The audience started to take their seats for the second act. I seized the moment. Carpe diem.

"You like cards?"

Ranier looked at me strangely.

"No. Not really."

I pulled a deck of cards from my jacket pocket. "I have a new hobby. Couldn't sleep on the flight and the onboard movies sucked."

The new security guards stepped forward. Ranier waived them off.

The two new guards spoke to the two guards who had led me to the box when I arrived. My Russian was very limited but I assumed they told the two new guys they had frisked me and were aware of the cards.

I opened the deck of cards and shuffled them. Ranier watched me curiously. I fanned the cards out and stated the age-old, "Pick a card any card."

"Are you serious?"

"Yes. I am. Just humor me."

Ranier hesitated then smiled. He put his wine glass down on the coffee table and reached over with his right hand. I moved toward his left to pull his attention further away from the wine glass. I leaned forward and with my left hand dropped the tiny clear tablet into his glass, which caused a small ripple but no audible noise.

Ranier picked a card and sat back. He quizzically stared at the card. A smile slowly formed and he started to laugh loudly.

He showed me the card as he continued to laugh. The card, the five of clubs, had the words "FUCK YOU!" written in all caps on it in black ink.

"I told you; it's only a hobby," I said as I put the cards back into the deck. I put the deck back into my jacket.

"Yeah. Don't quit your job."

"No shit."

The truth was that all of the cards had those words written on them. I needed a diversion and we wanted to keep it simple. Plus I thought it was funny under the circumstances.

Ranier was so arrogant, he didn't take it literally but rather thought I, a/k/a Leon Black, shared his cynical sense of humor. He'd soon know otherwise.

"Do I have time to hit the restroom?" I asked. "I really need to pee."

"Can't you make your piss disappear?" Ranier sipped his wine.

"You saw my card trick. What do you think?"

"Good point.

"Yeah. No problem. You can come and go as you please without interrupting anyone in a box."

"Great. I'll be right back."

As I got up to leave the bodyguards moved in front of me. Ranier waived them off. I nodded at Ranier. Then I paused and said, "When I come back, let's discuss whatever it is you want to tell me in person."

Ranier nodded, "Yep." He looked peaceful, turning his attention back to the stage. He sipped his wine again as I walked out.

I left the box and walked down the hall toward the theatre exit. Making my getaway. I would never know what it was he wanted to tell me.

Maybe he wanted to unburden himself. Maybe he'd identify others as part of some conspiracy. CIA never believed he acted alone.

Or maybe he just wanted someone to listen to him explain again why he did what he did. Like a therapy session.

Or maybe he wanted to share a recipe. Or some pathetic political diatribe.

Like I said, I'd never know. Nor would the Agency. Retribution was the objective and I assumed the Agency would be satisfied shortly.

As I walked out, I didn't regret my actions. Shortly after my departure, Ranier would notice a sudden runny nose and chest tightness. Soon after, he would start to drool, experience difficulty breathing and nausea would kick in. Then Ranier would start to loose control of his bodily functions. The textbooks and the Agency's briefing say the subject vomits, defecates and urinates followed by convulsions and suffocation. The whole thing would take approximately 20 minutes. And then ... well you get the idea.

I have to admit I'm glad I didn't stay to witness his demise. I preferred the shootout scenario. It seemed more honorable.

But as I said, I don't regret what I did. What were we supposed to do? Let a cynical, snot-nosed, arrogant little fuck lecture us incessantly while we waited for his doubtful extradition?

If the Russians ever agreed to extradition, it would come at a steep geopolitical price for our allies and us.

He put lives at risk as far as I was concerned. Our enemies, yes enemies, must laugh at our naivety. While they accelerate similar programs, we are dismantling ours and letting a self-described belligerent, self-important brat patronize our society. It was too much.

I understand the risks and need for close oversight of the data-mining program and I could reconcile that view with punishing a traitor who gave aid and comfort to our enemies. To not hold him accountable would only embolden further leaks and reckless actions in my estimation.

As I made my way to the exit, I noticed a female usher twenty-five feet or so ahead of me. Something about her seemed familiar. I slowed my pace. Breaking protocol, I made eye contact with her as I got closer.

Then I recognized her. It was Tracy.

She was wearing a black wig and glasses but I was certain it was her. I couldn't help but smile at her. Tracy smiled back but quickly turned to help a patron. Back in character. I remembered that she was fluent in Russian, French and Farsi.

As I exited the theatre, I fought back tears. Seeing Tracy was a relief. I thought she died a lonely death in the Bozeman café. I was so grateful she was OK.

It was strange. Despite our intense physical relationship when we first met, I felt no attraction for Tracy. Just respect and admiration. Tracy was a strong woman. A bad ass who I shared the foxhole with. She was a professional who practiced her craft amongst the deadliest of the sharks.

I think of her often. I just want Tracy to be safe and happy. She deserved that. Even if that meant I never saw her again.

As for Martha, it wasn't so simple. I felt like there was more to learn from Martha. She remained a mystery to me.

Martha could walk into any boardroom as CEO, Chairwoman, and Founder. She had the full package. Sophisticated beauty. Keen intellect. Confidence. An aura of competence. And a steely toughness that belied her feminism.

I exited the Kolobov Theatre and broke into the crisp evening air. Dirty, leaven-like snow covered the ground. I waived down a taxi and used my extremely limited Russian. 'Prinyat' do aeroporta.' Take me to the airport in English.

My transportation was to be as follows: private jet to Helsinki; commercial to London; then private back to US.

As I got into the cab. I looked back at the theatre. A yellow glow of light illuminated the foyer, which contrasted starkly with the black night outside.

The taxi pulled away. I pictured Ranier one last time. The peaceful look on his face. I momentarily felt bad for his

parents and even him. Was it dangerously misguided naivety or
extreme, consequence-be-damned arrogance? Whatever the case,
truth be told, I hoped he went quick and didn't have to suffer
badly. A double-tap would have been more humane.

It took months before it became public. An innocuous report on a
busy news day. Ranier, the infamous leaker had died due to
apparent natural causes. Official line was an asthma attack.
Even though there was no concrete evidence of childhood asthma,
the storyline was that he had developed the condition after
smoking unfiltered cigarettes for several months and exposure to
the polluted Moscow air.

The media even speculated that Russia killed him in return for
our cooperation on any number of geopolitical matters. No doubt
misinformation spread or at least welcomed by the Russians. The
other option – a hit right under their noses so-to-speak – was
too embarrassing to contemplate. Stateside, some speculated that
nefarious elements of the military-industrial complex killed
Ranier to preempt a presidential pardon.

I'm not aware of any video evidence of the job but I pictured
our self-righteous antagonist staring at the playing card as he
writhed on the burgundy carpet in the box. Finally realizing
that it wasn't a cynical joke as he had so confidently thought
based on his paradigm of the world. Literally, the Agency and I
on behalf of the American people were saying FUCK YOU.

IT'S A WRAP (OR IS IT?)

Well, what more is there to say? How do I feel? I feel great.

Did I trade my morals for a cure? Or did I take advantage of an opportunity to serve my country and protect my fellow Americans and our allies? I'm not sure.

I guess the litmus test is whether I'm proud of what I did. And yes, I am proud. I'd do it again.

But sometimes I'm nagged by whether I've committed grave sins for which I haven't sought forgiveness. For which I'm not sorry. Am I going to hell?

I don't know. Maybe the whole thing was a dream. I've read about intense, multi-day hallucinations that open-heart surgery patients experience post-op.

Maybe I've been hallucinating. Instead of sipping a beer on a Croatian beach listening to Steve Earle's <u>When I Fall</u>, maybe I'm in the hospital receiving a powerful chemical cocktail through a port.

Or maybe I'm in Purgatory. Maybe I didn't escape. Maybe the Russians killed me.

Or maybe CIA killed me. Would they really trust me not to tell my story? It's too crazy to be true. Or is it?

NOTES

I apologize for any spelling errors, incorrect grammar, etc. As an unauthorized memoir, I didn't have the help of an editorial staff. For what it may lack in polish, I'm hoping the rawness of my story makes it more relatable.

If you're wondering why I didn't share my story with the media, simple answer is I don't trust them. In my estimation, the so-called Fourth Estate is the most hypocritical institution in America. Even more morally bankrupt than the United States Congress, which is a difficult achievement.

Final note: I've acted alone in sharing my story. If there are any repercussions, I bare sole responsibility. I'm using my official code name because there's no point in trying to hide my identity from the Agency. The details I'm sharing ensure the Agency will know who wrote this story. However, I have changed names and some details to protect the lives of my colleagues. I admire them and am sharing this story to shine a light on their selfless efforts to protect us from our enemies -- both real and imagined. I'm also sharing my story to provide average Americans like me with a glimpse of the privilege and honor it has been to help protect innocent Americans as well as our friends and allies. God bless America.